A Man Named Ezell

A. J. Miller, Ph.D

First published by Dog Ear Publishing
4011 Vincennes Rd
Indianapolis, IN 46268
www.dogearpublishing.net

ISBN: 978-1-4575-6227-3

This book is printed on acid-free paper.

Printed in the United States of America

ACKNOWLEDGEMENTS

This book is dedicated to my Uncle John Oldham, to my family, and to my wonderful friends who helped me in so many different ways.

I would like to acknowledge the dear friend who encouraged me to write a book about the stories I told him weekly over dinner. Without Saverio Guadiano, this book would have never existed.

My daughter, Retta Donono, was very helpful and encouraging, as were my two sons, John and Kevin Curran.

My friend Ron MacKenzie deserves all the credit I can give him for his helpfulness and deep caring.

Another dear friend, Susie Hebert, typed the entire manuscript out of the goodness of her heart and was helpful in numerous other ways.

Brent Coleman, great author and historian, knew and supplied information and pictures of the time period in and around Aberdeen, Prairie, Monroe, and Lowndes Counties in Mississippi. I also thank him for the personal tour, for without him, we would never have found our way.

To Terry Fischer and Bill Kendrick, wonderful people who were so helpful and interested, all I can say is a grateful and humble "Thank you."

I actually knew and loved Ezell, Uncle John, Aunt Nettie, and many other characters in this book. Many of the situations were based upon reality, with a few of the conclusions fictionalized; therefore, the book is a "somewhat true story."

Ezell's death is now recorded on a headstone in a county churchyard in Lowndes County, Mississippi.

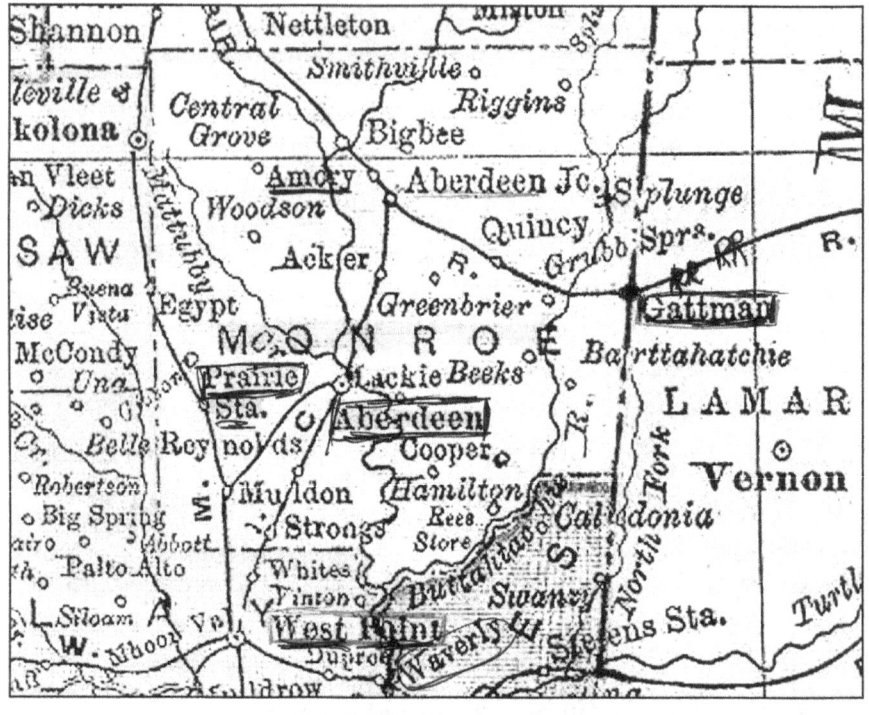

This old map shows northeast Mississippi, the names of the communities and small towns that existed before Ezell was born in 1920. It is the Deep South, the setting for this story. This was his stomping ground— the fertile, flat land of tall grasses and lush trees, of river bottoms, of lakes and streams … his land, love, and life.

The real people in Ezell's world were Uncle John, Aunt Nettie, Baby Girl, Annie, Rose, and Billy. Unfortunately, photographs of all these people no longer exist; if they ever did. Monroe County is where he played, learned, worked, courted, loved, and finally married his beloved Rose. It was the place they reared their children and called home. These are the people and the places that populate Ezell's story.

Ezell Jefferson Oldham

Mother Lauretta Patterson Hollis

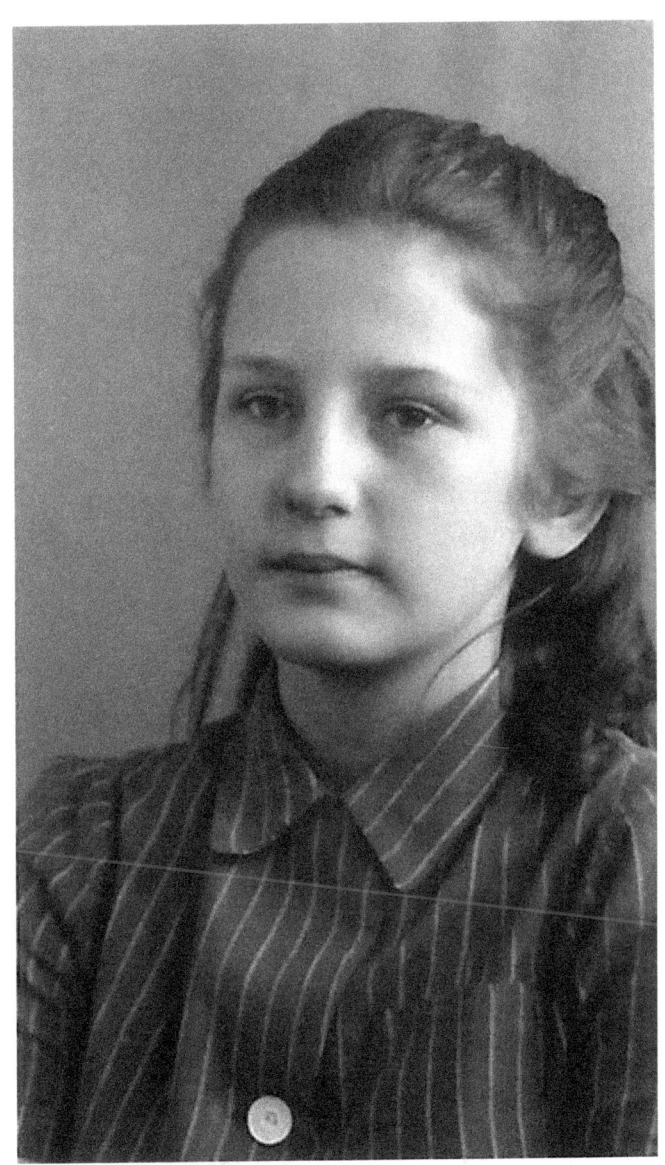

Baby Girl at seven

Uncle John Oldham

Auntie Nettie Oldham

Baby Girl, Jo at fourteen

1936

I think just hearing the story made me love Ezell before I ever met him. Uncle John told it so many times, and always in the same way, and with the same amount of wonder. I practically knew the story by heart.

"Hunching down closer to my horse, pulling my overcoat tighter to my body and bracing myself for the bitterly cold, iced-over Mississippi morning, I mounted Big Ben and headed out for the plantation to check on the workers' houses," he'd begin.

"The wind was blowing hard, sideways from the north. In fact, it was the coldest morning on record for the state of Mississippi … ten degrees below zero. December 23, 1920. The very day I came upon a frozen woman and a starving newborn.

"Just as I rounded the corner of the first one of the workers' houses, I heard what sounded like a baby crying, though so distressed and so faint that I wasn't even sure that this was what I heard. Nevertheless, I knocked on the door several times, actually pounded on it for the last few times, but nobody came. Only the water slid down and off the roof, freezing and forming icicles as it fell. At that time, I thought the best thing to do was break the door down. So I threw all my weight against the wooden door; it fell inward with a popping crash at the same time a loud clap of thunder intensified both sounds. I almost lost my best horse, Big Ben, but he quickly recovered from the noise and gave a snort as if to say, 'I've heard worse than that before.' That seemed to be Big Ben's attitude toward most everything."

Uncle John would pause here just to see if I was still listening and then go on. "With the door open, I entered," he'd say. "Oh my! I just about lost my breakfast … There, a frozen woman lay, very pale and extremely cold to the touch. When I gently pressed my hands against her eyes to close them, I noticed that she was wearing a cotton house dress with nothing much else on. Everything else she might have worn was placed around the baby: her coat, sweater, and the rest of her clothes, as well as a thin blanket and some men's clothing.

"Dear Lord, I prayed, please let her know her baby is alive. How she must have loved that little one. I picked up the little boy baby who was lying next to his dead mother for who knows how many days. I couldn't help but wonder if any of this would register in his little brain and if so, what it would do to him later in his life.

"From the neighbors I learned the mother had named him Ezell and that she had been a bit puny since the father had left them. None of the neighbors wanted the baby, either, and they said there were no relatives. I looked down at that little baby and thought, here he is in this world with no mother, no father, no kinfolk, and with all these people around him, and nobody wants him? Well, by God, I do!"

Then Uncle John would stop and excuse himself.

"Excuse me, Baby Girl, your Uncle John did wrong to take the Lord's name in vain ... Don't ever do that. The Lord forgives, but your Aunt Nettie might not, and other folks wouldn't like you anymore, either."

But he wasn't really sorry for telling the story that way and he would just take up where he left off.

"I walked out of that cabin with the little bundle of hungry baby in my arms, I'll have to admit, I had tears rolling down my face, thinking of what he must have been through and what he would have to go through later in life, even if your Aunt Nettie would let me keep him."

That's when I'd cry out. "Poor baby Ezell. His mother must have died of a broken heart."

"Poor baby Ezell *nothing!*" Uncle John would say and he'd look stern. "He went from a tenant house to one of the finest homes in Monroe County with more love heaped on him than anybody ever did. I was there, and I wanted him."

Uncle John would put a big smile on his face. "Since it was alright with the neighbors, I put Ezell up on Big Ben, and we rode off toward the house. Me wondering the whole time how your Aunt Nettie was going to take this.

"At first, she wouldn't even speak to me, and you can bet I was plenty worried. I explained everything to her, and she still wouldn't speak to me. She would just look at baby Ezell's face, then look at mine, as if she was trying to compare us to each other. I kept telling her that since I couldn't have children, because of being injured in the war, and we both wanted them so badly, this must be God's way of making it up to us. After a while, she came around, though.

"Baby Ezell just kept smiling and cooing at her until her heart melted," Uncle John would say. "One day I walked into our bedroom, and there she was, holding, rocking, and singing to baby Ezell."

I think just hearing Uncle John tell me that story made me love Ezell before I ever saw him. And it certainly caused me to have that sense of family for all of us, even though it was years before I finally got to meet Ezell for myself.

CHAPTER ONE

Life with Ezell and the Oldhams

*S*ince Saturday was the day off for all the farm workers and a much lighter day for Uncle John, he promised to let me ride on a gentle horse with him down to the lake. When he was supervising the workers, he rode his shiny black horse, Big Ben, to work each day over the plantation. Big Ben seemed to know that it was his day off too. Prancing and dancing around, with his tail flickering, he was in high spirits while heading down to the lake to walk into the water and drink.

The horse I rode was in stark contrast to Big Ben. Nell was a small matte-gray horse, very calm and quiet. She walked down to the lake up to her belly, causing me to hold my short, stubby little legs straight out so my shoes and socks didn't get wet. The lake smelled of sweet honeysuckle and the wildflowers growing in the field that surrounded it. Here and there was a little grove of pine trees and a few live oaks the cows used for shade. They stopped and watched the horses go down into the lake while they stood around the edges, extending their heads out and lapping water up with their tongues. Watching the minnows swim around in the shallow water was fun too. I always thought the horses would swallow a few minnows, but they never did. After the horses had their fill, they climbed up and over the bank onto the surrounding flat-as-a-pancake grassy field. What a relief it was to put my legs down again.

After this, we headed back to the house, which overlooked the lake and the fields. Its name was Lenoir. It was a beautiful house, indeed. Along the front porch, the house had tall white Doric columns. Down each side of the house were two more porches with smaller columns, and there were several chimneys that could be easily seen from the lake. The shutters were painted green, the architectural style was colonial revival of a classical design. I learned all of this from Aunt Nettie, who took Ezell and me on field trips. Each year, we went to several different places in Mississippi to learn the history of our state and a great deal about the architectural styles. We also learned about the architects and builders of the beautiful homes that were still left standing in West Point, Columbus, Aberdeen, Natchez, and even Vicksburg. They were all so different from the other, but each was breathtaking to both Ezell and me. The three of us enjoyed those field trips and learned much from them.

Historic home Natchez, Mississippi

Gazing at that big, beautiful house in Prairie, Mississippi, where my aunt, uncle, and Ezell lived was one of my favorite pastimes because I was dreaming of a house that I would live in some day. I would dream of wearing soft, flowing chiffon dresses and white gloves with a tall, handsome husband standing beside me. Then I would tell myself, "I can't have all of that, though, unless I marry a rich man or go to school for a very long time, like Aunt Nettie did." She went all the way through college and became a teacher. I decided then and there that I would do the same because it would let me keep on doing what I loved doing. I wouldn't run the risk of getting married to a man who might not want me to keep on being myself, nor like living with a strong-willed person, like I was.

When we got back to the house, the workers were all lined up at the side porch, which went directly into Uncle John's office. He sat at his desk in the little carved wooden chair (which I still have today) to write the checks. Unlike many field workers in that time and at other plantations, these workers were paid well enough to have some money left over at the end of the week.

When the check-writing was over around noon, Uncle John went into the dining room for lunch. Annie was the only worker who didn't get off until Saturday afternoon. Aunt Nettie and I cleaned up the kitchen and washed the dishes so Annie could leave as quickly as possible. Aunt Nettie always saw to it that Annie received something extra every Saturday, like a nice new-looking purse or a pretty hat or something else in which she had expressed an interest. These were the times after the Great Depression, and cash was scarce, so people often used things to replace money. This always made me happy because I could tell that Aunt Nettie was just as pleased to be able to give something nice as Annie was to get it. Three happy females …

Uncle John always said he "looooved happy women," so it must have made him feel good too. I think he loved us all the time, anyway, because he was always smiling with that big, broad smile of his and telling us how proud we made him feel.

As soon as Annie left, I knew it was time to go to town. All day Friday and Saturday morning, I looked forward to this. Uncle John had already told me that Ezell was going to town with us, and I was delighted to be with another young person. Ezell regarded me very much like Uncle John did, as if I were a little princess. After all, Aunt Nettie dressed me nicely, as if I actually were one.

Ezell had the little blue 1935 Ford ready to go to the town of Aberdeen. Of course, Uncle John and Aunt Nettie sat in the front, and Ezell and I sat in the back seat. Because the weather was getting very warm, I was sweating in my stiff organza dress, ruffled panties, white socks, and black patent-leather shoes. Aunt Nettie was, I'm sure, uncomfortable in her stiff dress and new silk nylon stockings. Uncle John and Ezell didn't seem to be suffering as much, because they were used to being out in the sun all day long. Farming was never easy in the sweltering, insect-ridden Deep South, where the temperature had gone as low as -10 degrees up to 110 degrees, and the summer lasted around five months a year.

By the time I met Ezell, he was a kind, well-educated teenager. He also had a very good vocabulary and was polite. As I later came to realize, it was partly because my Aunt Nettie had spent many hours each day teaching him. According to Aunt Nettie though, he was simply super bright. In those days, there was not a word for homeschooling. I had never met a person before in all my years that was anything like Ezell. In addition, our cook, Annie, made sure Ezell ate three good meals a day so he would be strong and healthy. Ezell was larger than the other boys of his age on the plantation and, of course, stronger.

Once, Ezell confided in me that he owed a "great debt" to my Aunt Nettie and Uncle John, who brought him up and gave him every opportunity that they would have given to their own son.

"How will you repay them?" I asked.

With a great deal of determination in his voice and an expression that I had never seen before on his face, he clearly and simply said, "I'll find a way!" And without a doubt in my mind, I knew he would.

It was amazing just how much ridicule Ezell seemed to be able to tolerate from some of the white, as well as the black, boys and girls in and around the plantation. He never seemed to get angry and never allowed anyone to push him into a fight. Aunt Nettie had drilled that into his head: "Smart boys don't have to fight; they don't have to because they are intelligent enough and know how to say the right things." And "no one can fight a person who refuses to fight with them." She even did some role-playing situations with him so he would know exactly what to say and do. She would conclude their sessions with statements like "Just because someone says bad things about or to you, does not make it true." Then she would end with "Now you say it."

When I asked him how he was able to ignore so much, he would just smile and say, "They really don't know any better. Someday, they may be my friends, and many will walk up and offer their hand to me and sincerely apologize. So, don't you think we can forgive them, Baby Girl?"

Sometimes I had the idea that underneath, Ezell was seething with an anger that had been with him so long, he couldn't pinpoint its beginning. Only Uncle John knew about that.

"So, don't you think we can forgive them, Baby Girl?" This was Ezell's first attempt at trying to teach me the power of forgiveness. Looking back, it was at this point that I realized "poor baby Ezell" had grown into a man wise beyond his years and was trying to teach me to be a better person than he was.

How Ezell looked forward to the plantation school, too, especially when he got older and there was a smart and pretty new teacher there. He must have graduated three times before one of the teachers caught on and asked him if he wasn't a little old to still be in school. He got away with it as long as he did because one or two of the other boys were behind in school and were older than the other students.

"I'll bet Ezell is going to follow one of those teachers to Starkville someday," I said.

Uncle John told me that Ezell had run away a few times and maybe that was why I said what I did, or maybe it was a premonition, because that was exactly where Ezell spent many of the later years in his life.

Uncle John was a tall, tanned, and pleasant-looking man. He was the descendent of a family in Tennessee who owned a ranch and raised Tennessee walking horses. When the parents died, they passed all they had down to Uncle John and his brother, so Uncle John had owned a plantation and horses himself until he came back from fighting in France during World War I. While he was away, his brother Ned took over the business and lost everything. When Uncle John came back from the war, the plantation was no longer his.

Aunt Nettie relayed the story to me like this: In 1919, when the train rolled into Aberdeen, Mississippi, Uncle John received a telegraph: "No need to come home. *Stop.* Susan now married. *Stop.* Horses and land gone too. *Stop.* Ned."

It still brings tears to my eyes just to think about how sad that must have been for my uncle. Coincidentally, this was also the day Aunt Nettie met Uncle John. Aunt Nettie told me that she met the train in Aberdeen that day, and she spotted a soldier walking around with tears in his eyes. He seemed so disheartened that she couldn't stand it, so she went over to him and said, "Soldier, you look so sad even though you are back on the soil of the country you loved so much that you were willing to give up your life for her. She is still free because of that. Is there anything I can do that would help you?"

Uncle John later told me that this was when he realized what he still had, at that time. He had his own life, his country and its freedoms, and this kind and caring woman who wanted so much to help him. He saw her compassion, heard her sweet, soft voice, and realized that her beauty was inside, as well as out. The next thing out of his mouth was "Yes, beautiful lady, you can marry me. Will you?"

To his great astonishment, Aunt Nettie, who had also looked into his heart, smiled at him and said, "Yes! Now, my dear husband-to-be, by what name shall I be called?"

"Why, 'Mrs. Oldham,'" Uncle John said, rather surprised because of the delightful way she had asked her question to learn his name.

Aunt Nettie later told me that they both laughed all the way back to the teachers' home where she was boarding. Aunt Nettie was tall and slender and always wore soft, flowing dresses of the latest fashion. She was a graceful and beautifully spoken Southern lady. My Uncle John had the bearing of a confident, aristocratic gentleman.

It was obvious to all the people they got to know in Aberdeen that they were very much in love. Each of them felt they were the luckiest of all people in just meeting the other, then falling in love, and it showed in so many different ways.

Not long afterward, Uncle John got a job as a plantation manager in Prairie, Mississippi. They made a striking couple and had a quiet little wedding there in the beautiful mansion in which they were to live. Lenoir Mansion survived, and it is just as beautiful now as it was in 1847 when it was built by the Lenoir family of Texas.

Lenoir Mansion

Uncle John used his first paycheck to buy Big Ben, a Tennessee walking horse, and rode the beautiful, shiny black stallion over the plantation every day, except the weekend. He also entered him in local horse shows, where Big Ben won more trophies and blue ribbons than I knew how to count (until I got into the second grade). A few months after that, Uncle John found the perfect horse for my aunt to ride, along with a fine leather side-saddle. Aunt Nettie named her horse Love's Gift, but called her Love, like she did Uncle John.

It was another year after this, in 1920, that Uncle John found a starving little black boy, Ezell. And I, I was the little white girl who loved them all …

Saturday again, and every Saturday we went to Aberdeen for the week's supplies—the animals' and our own. Again, the little blue 1935 Ford ran over the deeply rutted gravel roads caused by the winter rain and occasional snowstorms. Dust flew as we traveled over the bumpy roads. When we got almost a mile outside of Aberdeen, the road became paved. And, oh my, that was so nice. As we pulled up onto the main street of town, I saw two white men standing together. They were shaking their fists at us, but to my embarrassment, not at us but at Ezell! I told him that I was sorry they were acting like that. Covering his embarrassment and anger, Ezell smiled and nodded to me in acknowledgment. Then he quietly said, "Baby Girl, that doesn't bother me. I understand that many of our prejudices are like pyramids upside down; they rest on one tiny incident, but they spread upward and outwards until they fill our minds. The less secure a man is, the more likely he is to have extreme prejudices."

I asked, "What are 'pyramids'?"

"Now I'm sorry," Ezell said. "I was not talking very well to you, Baby Girl, and tomorrow afternoon we are going to sit down and talk over all the things you have asked me about, and I'll make it easy for you to understand. Why, we might even build a pyramid out of that new clay you got! Then I'll show you what a pyramid looks like."

"Yeah," I said.

"You and I aren't going misunderstand each other because of some words and thoughts. We will come to understand the words we hear and use. Someday, Baby Girl, you will love learning just as much as I do; it will open many doors for both of us." Time would prove that Ezell was absolutely right …

Ezell seem to be trying very hard to rise above what we both had seen in Aberdeen. Later, when I got a little bit older, I talked with Ezell about this, and he told me why he was trying so hard to appear not to be bothered by it. Ezell said, "I don't like these feelings I have down deep in the pit of my stomach—of emptiness, not belonging in this world, of being less than I want to be, of feeling hurt, even angry. And I don't want you to feel that way when you have no reason to. I was afraid it would affect you, Baby Girl."

I said, "No, Ezell, the only one of those feelings I have that you do is anger. I get angry with people for acting so stupid, and then they try to teach other people to act stupid, too—for the rest of their life, maybe! Know what I believe, Ezell? That there's nobody better than I am, and … there is nobody less, either."

"That's pretty good, Baby Girl … Thanks for telling me that."

"Is it our secret then?"

"Yes, sirree!"

When we arrived at the center of town, our first stop was at the little drug store that Mr. McKenizie and his white-haired daughter owned. It had a tile floor with a black-and-white checkerboard pattern on it and a wonderful counter with round-top stools that fit up close. The stools would twirl all the way around and around again—if there were no adults with a mind to stop a little girl from having fun. Of course, there was a wonderful soda fountain and a very ornate carved mantle on the wall just above it. Mr. McKenizie would press a lever down, and out came the best ice cream in the whole world. Ezell was the one that bought the ice cream that day, with Uncle John standing there right behind us.

Ezell whispered to me, "No one will ever bother us with your Uncle John standing there with his feet planted apart and his hands on his hips and that look on his face. Look at him, Baby Girl. What do you see?"

"I see the big ole tall cowboy that I saw in last Saturday's movie," I said.

"And what did the cowboy look like and what did he say?" asked Ezell.

"He looked scary, even if he was one of the good guys, and he said, 'If any of you robbers takes one dollar out of the farmers' bank, you'll regret it for the rest of your short life, because I'll hunt you down and string you up, if it's the last thing I do.' "

I was so happy because I already had a feeling that there was nothing that I would like better than learning—unless it was eating ice cream like I was doing now.

Uncle John and Ezell left to go buy feed for the horses and cows, along with supplies for the farm, while Aunt Nettie and I shopped in the ready-to-wear for children and women. Seemed that I had outgrown my shoes and some of my dresses again. Though Aunt Nettie never outgrew anything, she always got something new every time she got something new for me. We finally got what we needed to be able to go to church, as well as a few things to help keep me entertained for the next week. Aunt Nettie insisted that my toys and books had to be educational.

Ezell and Uncle John had also finished getting all the supplies for the week, and they loaded them onto the carrier that was tied securely on top of the car. When they got in the car, we were ready to head back to Prairie—for home.

As we rounded the last curve to the farm and came near the plowed-up rows of soil, I could smell the rich, good black earth. Oh, how I loved that smell! Over in the pastures, some of the cows were lazily grazing away, while others were gathering under the shade trees to rest. About that time, Penny, the female bulldog, and her pup barked away, as if to say, "Welcome home," and they ran out to greet us. It was good to be back home where everything was calm and peaceful, where people were good to each other and even the animals seemed to welcome us.

Sunday morning, Aunt Nettie and I usually went to church. This particular Sunday, she was rushing me around like crazy. "Here, Baby Girl, get your socks pulled up. I can't do everything for you. Just because you turned seven is no excuse for you to dillydally around," Aunt Nettie said.

"Why, Aunt Nettie," I asked, "do we have to go to a different church from the First Methodist in town today? I like that one where the little red-haired girl went and where the children would play with me instead of standing around looking at me and wanting to touch my hair."

"I know," said Aunt Nettie, "but we received a special invitation to our church today, and if we aren't on time, they'll be waiting for us. So we have to hurry, and we have to look our very best."

"But, Aunt Nettie," I said.

"No 'buts' about it. Finish getting ready this minute, young lady. *Now!*"

All of this was being said as she was yanking up her corset, adjusting her broad-brimmed hat, and putting on lacy gloves. Then she began pulling me along the freshly waxed front hallway, out onto the endless front porch with the big white columns, down the brick steps and walkway, across the perfectly manicured lawn, to the awaiting car. "Quickly!" she said, putting me into Uncle John's little car and driving off.

After traveling down a narrow gravel road for less than a mile, we soon arrived at the church. It was a small wooden church with a big white cross right above the front door. It was well cared for and spotlessly clean.

"Now you put a smile on your face, missy." And then she admonished, "Do you hear me?"

"Yes, ma'am," I quickly said, for fear she would do something like box my jaws, as she had threatened on occasion before but had never done.

When we went through the door to the inside of the church, the first person that I saw was Ezell and then Pastor Finsen, who hand-motioned us to the front row, where there were two vacant seats.

"Ladies," Pastor Finsen said, "please sit here. We are pleased to have you here with us on this, our Lord's day."

About this time, the choir began to sing ever so softly and sweetly. I was gradually reduced to joy and contentment, and over time slowly laid my head down in Aunt Nettie's lap and drifted off to the beautiful sound of heavenly peace. When church was over, we went home. Aunt Nettie let Ezell drive the car so she could hold me, even though I was going on eight years old.

After church on Sunday, when we sat down at the table for our midday meal. Uncle John always pulled out the chair for Aunt Nettie, and Ezell did the same for me. Having good table manners and good conversation was really important to both Uncle John and Aunt Nettie. Because of this, Aunt Nettie would hold a short meeting between the two of us for the purpose of teaching me to know what to do and how to behave at the table. The first thing she taught me was the importance of setting a pretty, colorful table. We started by putting on a clean, freshly starched tablecloth and matching napkins. Sometimes, dollies were placed on the table, depending on our color scheme for the meal. Flowers, greenery, and/or some kind of centerpiece was a must; that was chosen from the colors used in the tablecloth or from the event. Napkin holders, glasses, and china all flowed together in a harmonious way. Conversation was light and positive.

Sundays were always Aunt Nettie's day to cook, because she wanted to prepare Ezell's and Uncle John's favorites. Uncle John grew up in Tennessee and liked different dishes from what we Mississippi people even knew about back then. Rhubarb pie was one of his favorites. Aunt Nettie questioned him about it until she learned how to make it just like his mother had. And she showed me how to do it, as well. "So, if a seven-year-old can make it, anyone can," my aunt said.

Sunday afternoon, just as Ezell had promised, we built a pyramid. It was just magnificent (a new word I learned that afternoon). Then we made a village nearby and put a few other things around it that would have been there at the time in history. Such fun! Right after Ezell repaired my doll's head and replaced her voice box, he told me that he not only liked building things but that he enjoyed making objects work and repairing broken things so they would work again. Uncle John always said that Ezell could fix anything. And he was so glad, because he didn't have the time to repair all of the farm equipment, supervise the workers, and do the bookkeeping too. "Horses and people, I know," he would say, "but not machinery."

Most of the summers were much the same. The main difference was that Ezell began to leave the plantation for a month or so, sometimes longer, as he grew older. This went on for several years until 1942, in fact, until Ezell reached twenty-two years of age. This time, he returned to ask Uncle John and Aunt Nettie for their blessing for him to enlist in the military. As his adopted parents, he wanted their blessing at this important step in his life. Ezell also wanted Uncle John to know he wanted to enlist to do what Uncle John had done to help his country. Of course, they gave him their blessing, but Aunt Nettie cried for several days before she put up the blue star, which symbolized parents whose sons were serving their country, in her window.

CHAPTER TWO

First Trip on the Train

By now you may be wondering why my parents would allow me to go all summer for so many summers to visit my Aunt and Uncle. It seems that in the summer of 1936 and during the rest of that year, out of boredom and curiosity, I "outdid" myself and the patience of my parents. It really upset my mother to no end that I was barely six years old and had been caught in my first attempt at smoking cigarettes. My best friend, Betty, and I had chosen the outhouse as our hiding place, but when I heard my mother coming out of the back door of the house, I knew she was headed toward us. "We have to get rid of these cigarettes," I said. "Hide them under all those Sears and Roebuck catalogs."

Of course, this resulted in a rapidly burning fire, and my friend and I ran out of the outhouse with our underwear down. We just pretended we had been answering nature's call while the flames blazed away. The outhouse was soon reduced to a pile of ashes. The result was that my daddy had to build an indoor bathroom in order to placate my mother about the whole fiasco.

Daddy was even more perturbed when I caught a passing freight train but was not able to jump off before it gained speed again. Therefore, I had to hang on until the train stopped in the next town six miles away. There, I walked to the police station to call my father to come pick me up. He had to close the grocery store and service station to do it, and needless to say, I was in bad trouble. Not nearly as bad, though, as when my cousin and I got bored waiting in the car for Daddy and decided to liven things up by "mooning" some of the townspeople. (I really don't want to talk about that one anymore; it's embarrassing.)

We were both in bad trouble. This last incident had been so humiliating to my father that he told us, after using a razor strap on both our bottoms, that he didn't know if he could ever show his face in Sulligent again during his lifetime. I felt the same way, too, because I thought I would always be afraid someone would come up to me when I was a grown woman and say, "Oh, you were that little Hollis girl who started the mooning craze way back." Just the thought of it made me cover my face in shame.

Mother and Daddy put their heads together and decided that what I needed was something to keep me occupied. Since the service station was connected to the grocery store and Daddy didn't have anyone working in the service station, he decided that I could bring the gas money to him in the grocery store when change was necessary. I could pump the gas when it was needed, which was all well and good, but my father did not take into consideration how those big, burly farmers would not take to a little girl pumping gas for them. They did not like it one little bit, and I was out of a job just about as fast as my little dog, Wimpie, could eat hamburger meat.

Now what to do? Well, before I got out of bed early one morning,

Tenant houses, Prairie, MS, 1930

which was always when my mother and father had their arguments (they thought that I couldn't hear them in my bedroom, but I could), they were talking about my Aunt Nettie and Uncle John wanting children but not being able to have them. Mother said, "You know they adopted that little colored boy that lost his mother, though. Do you think that will make any difference?" Daddy quickly spoke up, "Of course it won't! Who wouldn't want a nice, quiet white child instead of a colored one? If we sent Alva Jo for the summer, they would move him out to one of the field workers' houses. You know that Alva Jo won't like him." Then Mother quietly said, "Woodie, I wouldn't count on that. I hear the boy is a very good child and works hard keeping all the farm machinery running, and Nettie told me herself that they both loved him. Not only does she think he is smart but she thinks that he was God's gift to them, because that was what John told her the day he brought him home."

Stomping his foot, Daddy said, "I don't believe that for a minute, Loretta. Now that is enough. She is going."

"Yeah!" I yelled under my breath.

Boy, oh boy, tomorrow I was going to take a train on the inside for the first time ever … Wonder if I would have to hold on real tight? I sure did when I was hanging on to the caboose and riding through town before I jumped off … Wonder if the inside people would smile at me like some of the people in the caboose did? Sometimes, though, they just waved their arms and hands back and forth real fast, and their faces got all scrunched up, and their mouths went up and down like they were try-ing to yell something to me. If they could have just yelled louder than the train whistle was blasting out, I would have known what they were trying to tell me. Betcha they were just wishing me a fun day.

Now, what to take with me? Mother would tell me to take whatever I wanted, but I was too old to take my favorite doll, Polly Peach-Tree. So, I just took some pants, shirts, and my high-tops … Wonder if there would be anything to eat and how long it would take to get to Aberdeen … Guess I better stuff those things in my suitcase now, because we'll have to get up early, and there'll not be time to do it then …

It was morning. The sun was in my eyes, and it was time to get up. I heard my mother yell to hurry and get dressed because breakfast was ready. Then it was hurry through breakfast … It was always hurry, hurry,

hurry to do something around here …

That very morning, Mother and Daddy told me that I could go spend the summer with Aunt Nettie and Uncle John. Of course, I acted very "surprised," as well as pleased. On Sunday, Mother and Daddy took me to Sulligent, where the train stopped before going on to Aberdeen. Aunt Nettie and Uncle John would be there to meet me. *Maybe Ezell might be there, too*, I thought hopefully. I had always heard good things about him when Uncle John and Aunt Nettie would come to visit Mother, her sister.

Then it was time to get into the car and head to Sulligent six miles up a gravel road … Bye, Wimpie, bye little house, bye chickens. In no time, we were at the train station, and I was lifted up and into the passenger car. I quickly found a window seat and barely had time to wave goodbye to Mother and Daddy when the whistle blew two short blasts. Then the car jolted forward and off we went through clouds of steam and smoke. I was scared and did not know why. Maybe it was because I didn't know anyone in the car. I was alone and felt alone for the first time in my life. I wanted my mother, and I wished I had brought Polly Peach-Tree to hold onto. I had to do something fast to get over the feeling, because I knew no one was going to do it for me. What to do? I always got my mind off of everything else when I was reading and looking at interesting pictures. I had just the thing on the big shelf above my head. To reach up that high, however, would take more than just my standing up; I would have to stand up in my seat to get my suitcase down while the car was bouncing along the tracks, and it was pretty unsteady doing so.

I heard a man say, "Little girl, may I help get your suitcase down?"

"Oh, no sir, I don't need any help. I do this all the time … reaching up and pulling things down that are over my head. You see, there are some apples in a tree across the road from my house, and I go over there and pull the apples down by reaching high. My mother is always telling me, though, 'The Federal Land Bank is going to get you.' I never saw anyone with that name, but he's got to be mean with a name like that. He, or whatever it is, doesn't want me to get the apples off of his tree, or he

Aberdeen Depot

wouldn't be trying to get me! I do watch out for someone or something to catch me every time I go over to pick those apples. I even tell myself 'The Federal Land Bank is going to get you,' but it doesn't stop me. So, you see, I really don't need any help, but I thank you for asking."

"Little girl, you may not need anyone to help you, but you really do need to learn to not talk so much. You could have simply told me, 'No, thank you.' "

"Mister, I am talking so much because I am scared, and I feel like I have a big hole in my stomach, and I thought talking to you might make it go away."

"Here, little girl, I'm going to pull that suitcase down for you anyway and put it in the seat beside you. After you finish, you can just slide it under your seat. I do admire your independent spirit and determination, though."

"Thanks," I said, feeling so much better knowing that he did not want me to fall and get hurt.

I read and looked at pictures of Flash Gordon in his beautiful red-and-gold suit for quite a while until things flying by my window caught my attention. Trees were going by so fast that I could not even count them, but I could tell they were tall, had lots of branches, and were bright green. Such pretty colors, more than one shade with a soft-looking brown bark. When my daddy was in the lumber business, they were what he called loblolly pines. Daddy was always looking at the woods and trees as lumber. I had a great fondness for the woods and trees and did not want them cut down, partly because a large number of animals depended on them for their cover and their food.

Every time the train slowed down and stopped in a small town, there was the loud noise of the train's whistle, the screeching of the brakes, and the sound of the wheels as they rolled over the rails. Then, for a moment or two, everything was quiet … blessed silence like the woods, until a new group of people bounded up into the train. Then we started up the same way again: loud whistle, screeching brakes, and the sound of the wheels clattering over and over again. Loud noises always scared me, but this was an exciting adventure, I told myself.

Pastures, cows and horses, farmland, grasses, and towns were seen in rapid succession. Occasionally, the train would slow down enough for a man to leave a bag and, sometimes, take a bag of mail at a train station as we went by. In each case, an extended pole with a hook on the end was used to catch the bag as we passed by. In some cases, the man in the baggage car would simply toss the bag, if it was small, to a waiting man on the station's platform. Once in a while, they tossed it both ways, and they must have been very good, because they never missed—not while I was on the train, anyway.

A man went through the cars announcing the names of the town in which we passed through or stopped. Before too many hours passed, I heard him call out, "Aabbeerrddeenn," and I began to get ready to get off. Before long, we pulled into the large railroad station on the outskirts of the town. I could see a little blue Ford car and Uncle John and Aunt Nettie waiting for me.

After arriving in Aberdeen and greeting Uncle John and Aunt Nettie,

I asked where Ezell was. Uncle John laughingly told me, "He is at the schoolhouse, graduating again before the smart, young teacher leaves for college."

"Why does she need to go to college again, Uncle John?" I asked.

"So she can teach in other schools, rather than just the plantation ones," Uncle John said. "The teachers are somebody with whom Ezell can carry on an intelligent conversation, and that is important to him. He said to tell you that he would make it up to you in a few days."

The trip had been more tiring for me than I realized it would be, and by the time I got to Prairie and into the lovely home, I was ready to get my bath and go to bed for the night.

The next day, I met Ezell. Right away, I knew he was going to be just as busy helping run the plantation as Uncle John was, and keeping about the same hours. Aunt Nettie and I did other things during the day to keep busy, have fun, and help "the men" out too. The first day I was there, she took me to the big library in Aberdeen to get some books for my age and reading level. The sweet lady librarian, Miss Peacock, knew just how to help us find some really good books, and I was able to check out an armful to take home for two whole weeks—in my own name too. Aunt Nettie wanted to visit one of her friends in town who had a sweet little girl named Mary about my age, and we had a wonderful time there too. Later, Aunt Nettie let me settle in at home with my new books while she prepared what she called "lesson plans" for what Ezell was studying from one until three o'clock each day. When I asked her if she would do that for me, too, she was delighted and said we would begin a program by next Monday beginning at 9:30 a.m. sharp and ending at 10:00 for three weeks. Then she said that if I felt like I wanted to continue with it, we would develop one for the next three weeks at the same beginning time, but maybe going until eleven o'clock. We both had to agree on it though. I thought it was really nice that I was going to get to make a decision about what I was going to do about learning important things, and even what I thought was important to know. *Wow! Aunt Nettie must think I'm smart—or I'm going to be, one day. I like that a lot!*

After I told Ezell all about my asking Aunt Nettie to teach me, too, and what had come of that, he told me he was going to get to make a big decision soon too. He seemed so excited about his recent conversation with his friend, Billy Pogue, and his trip to West Point, Mississippi, that he talked to me quite a while about. It was really important to Ezell's life—so important that he asked me not to tell anyone who would wish to cause any pain to Aunt Nettie and Uncle John or a Mr. Paul Jefferson. I never did, either.

CHAPTER THREE

Is This My Dad?

*E*zell's decision started the rock rolling. All kinds of stuff that led to a whole bunch of things that only Ezell could tell and do right by. I learned most of it later, but this is Ezell's story and told in his own words.

Billy and I were talking one morning about some work he had done in the nearby town of West Point. "So, Billy, you spent some time in our little town of West Point working for somebody by the name of Paul. Paul who?" I asked.

"Paul Jefferson," Billy replied. "Because my dad made a saddle for him, he wanted me to come over and work on the stirrups. When I finished, he paid me lots more than it was worth. Wish I knew why."

"Maybe he felt guilty about something between your dad and himself. I don't know, Billy, but that was my father's name too. Of course, there could have been another person by the same name, but it's unlikely. I'm just wondering … Think I'll go over there, knock on the door, and find out for myself. Tell me how to find the house, Billy."

"Okay, Ezee, I'll tell you, but first, you tell me how that's gonna do you, or anybody else, any good. This Mr. Jefferson has got hisself a lot of chillen and a nice wife too."

"I'll try to tell you how it might do some good, Billy, but right now I'm not sure it will, either. Anyway, I plan to be nice about everything. If it is my father, I won't be hitting him in the face that he ran away and left Mother and I to die. He might not have even known about me, though, for all I know."

"That's good, Ezee. I was thinking you might, just might, accuse the man, and he maybe had a reason for doing what he did."

"What kind of reason could a man have of going off and leaving a woman to die?" I asked, with that old anger rising in the pit of my belly.

"*See*, there you go Ezee! You think this over, and then maybe I'll tell you how to find Mr. Jefferson."

"It's a deal, Billy."

That night, I went to my room early to do some thinking about what Billy had asked me. I thought, *I know I've had a problem since I was a little boy. Neither colored nor white have ever accepted, or even liked me, partly because I was seen as a mix of the two races. I'm not! I'm colored! Both my mother and my father were colored, so I can't be a mix. I speak like white people because I've been brought up with them. My mama was a teacher, and she taught me my manners and many other things I would have never known. Mama and Papa have been good to me, but I haven't had a chance to find out what it would be like had I been brought up by my own kind of people. This might be my opportunity. If I could just visit with them, maybe the colored people would learn not to dislike me so much. Somehow, I've got to get this thing straightened out, and if Mr. Jefferson is my father, this might be a way. I just don't want to hurt Mama and Papa by telling them this, though. Maybe they don't realize that I'm hurt by people most every day. Yes, I know I'm trying to justify my actions, but my desire to belong has been so strong for so long that I almost feel that I have to do some-thing … So if I get a chance to visit with this family, I'm going to take it. I'll just leave here and not say anything about it. After all, I am almost a man now. I think that might be easier for them. I can swear Billy to secrecy. If he knows how important it is, he'll do it for me. So now I can talk to Billy and tell him what's on my mind. I know I'm being selfish, but I have to find out who I am. I'll tell Billy in the morning. Now for some sleep …*

I hoped I didn't oversleep, because Mama was making those great-tasting apple fritters she did every once in a while. She always told Papa and me that she was letting Annie sleep late on the mornings when she fixed us breakfast, but we knew better. Years ago, Papa told me that this was another way Mama showed her love for us.

I could smell that coffee and those fritters. After breakfast, I was going to look for Billy and tell him what I was going to do.

On the way over to West Point, I kept thinking about what I was going to say to Mr. Jefferson when he opened the door at his house, so I began to practice my greeting. When I finally got there and knocked on the front door, a boy who looked a great deal younger than I answered.

"Evening," the boy said, "you looking for somebody?"

"Well, I was hoping I could speak to Mr. Paul Jefferson," I said.

"Ain't here," the boy replied.

"Then when can I see him?" I asked.

"Whenever he gets back," said the boy.

"You don't talk much, do you? What's your name?"

"James. What's yours?"

"Ezell's my name … Ezell Jefferson."

"Sit down on those steps and wait."

"Thank you, James," I replied.

James went on back inside the house without further comment.

"That's kind of interesting," I said under my breath. "This kid is different—seemed like he couldn't wait to get back inside the house. I've never met anyone who used so few words in such a short period of time. Oh well, he isn't the kind of person I've run into most of my life."

At long last, it must have been Mr. Jefferson I saw coming down the road.

"Hello, my name is Ezell, and I've come from Prairie to talk with Mr. Paul Jefferson."

"You've come from aways then, young man. I see you've been sitting here waiting for me. I'm Jefferson. What is it that you walked this far to talk to me about?"

"You already know my friend Billy Pogue, I believe. He was telling me all about working for you and what a fine family you have over here. I just met your son James when I knocked on your door awhile ago."

"Oh, James, well he's the strange one—maybe I should just say different. He thinks he wants to go off to Georgia somewhere to college, to do 'Lord knows what.' One of his teachers is working with him on this idea too. Now isn't that something?"

"Yes, sir, surely is."

"So, what is you wanten to talk to me about?"

"Well, sir, I jus' wanted to run a little story by you to see what you thought about it," I said.

"A story ... then shoot. I like a good story."

"Okay, it goes like this. There was a colored man and woman who lived and worked on a plantation in Mississippi. Well, they were both young, strong, and in love with each other. They worked hard and thought everything was going very well for them until one day in December of 1920. This was when the husband told his wife he needed to go to the store to get some supplies and he would gather more firewood when he got back in a few hours. It was really cold that winter. It was so cold that it broke the historical record for the state of Mississippi for the coldest day ever recorded. Sir, it was 10 degrees below zero up in the northern part of the state in a little town named Ponotock. Here in Prairie, it hovered around 0 degrees most of the day. Now that's cold! Anyway, a big fire was roaring in the fireplace, and it nearly warmed the little one-room house. It was plenty good for cooking a big chicken too. So, chicken and dumplings was what the young couple were planning to have for supper that night ... chicken and dumplings, a little left-over pot liquor from collards, and some cornbread. Yes, sirree! So, the husband opened the door and walked out into the freezing weather. His wife didn't want him to go, but he told her that he had to go get 'em some supplies. He stepped back inside to give her a kiss goodbye. And he left again—never to return. His wife never saw him again, or he her, after that moment in time," I said. Then he added, "What made it even worse was that she was expecting a baby soon."

Dragging it out just a bit, I said, "The name of the plantation from which he left was Lenoir. Are you familiar with Lenoir, Mr. Jefferson? 1920?"

"Yes, I surely am. I used to work at Lenoir many years ago," Mr. Jefferson replied.

I was watching the expressions on Mr. Jefferson's face as I continued the story, but much more in-depth now. I was even looking right into the older man's eyes to see if there was a change in pupil size.

I kept going, but more slowly still ... "Yes, sir—Lenoir, back in the

'20s. The wife's name was Joy, and I heard she was a right pretty woman. Does this story have any special meaning to you, Mr. Jefferson?"

"Why, of course, it has meaning. She was a good woman, and she was a pretty woman too. I loved that woman, Lordy me, I loved her with every bone in my body. Tell me some more of your story, son; it's a good story, except for the part where I couldn't get back to her. She had chicken and dumplings cooking for that night, too, and there was always tantalizing looks coming from those 'talking eyes.' And, oh my, what that sweet little mouth would do. She was so special. She was all I could think about when I was away from her." He brought out a worn old sheet of paper. "This is a little poem that Joy's momma taught her when she was a child." In a faltering voice, he read:

> Now don't forget when things go wrong,
> To try the magic of a song.
> A cheerful heart and a smiling face
> Pours sunshine in the darkest place.

With my throat so tight I could hardly speak, I asked, "If she was that special and you loved her so much, then why didn't you come back to us?"

That was when Paul Jefferson, all 180 pounds of a grown man, completely broke down into great sobs that seemed to go on so long, I wondered if he would ever regain control of himself. Finally, after wiping his face and blowing his nose and clearing his throat numerous times, Mr. Jefferson was able to haltingly speak again. "By the time I could have got away, I had been gone too long. As pretty as she was, I figured she had gotten herself another man and wouldn't want me back by then. The cause was I couldn't get away, I couldn't! I was caught in a trap—a human trap, not a bear trap. I was treated like a slave, even though that should have been over a long time ago. They used me, worked me so hard that at times I wished I was dead. It went on so long that things got all mixed up in my head, and I began thinking crazy things. I was gone so long that I thought she would never want me back. I couldn't get away from them, I tell you. There were too many of them and only one of me. There was some really mean man there by the name of Luther Weamie or … something or other … too long ago. He was the one who had hired all of those men. He had a bunch of dogs with him, too, mean dogs that would hunt you down, no matter what you did to get them off your tracks. They were 'man-eaters' too. I heard they surrounded a man once, and this Luther gave them some sort of command. They jus' ate the man up like they had been about half-starved for that reason. Never know dogs would do that, but these would. They all looked like big ole wolves to me anyway."

I spoke up, "Maybe they were wolves, caught from those dark woods not too far away from Lenoir plantation."

"I'm afraid of those woods, too, but not as 'fraid of them as of the dogs," said Paul. "The woods around Prairie and Aberdeen are filled with the ghosts of a lot of our own kind of people, you know, Ezell, all the way back from the slave days. If a man or even an animal gets killed unexpectedly, or without anybody to bury him and say a few words over him, he's turned into a ghost right there on the spot. I heard that's why there's so many ghosts down there in those river bottoms around where the plantations were. There's panthers, too, and …"

"Mr. Paul, I want to talk some more about your wife's and my mom's life. About things I wouldn't know unless you or the white man who found me told me."

"Please, Ezell, I know now that you are my son and I'm your father, but I can't talk about that woman that was my whole life to me. I would have done anything for …"

And this was another time when Paul Jefferson broke down in great sobs. Crying for his lost love. When he finally could talk, he told me that she was so beautiful to him inside and outside that he even called her that for a while: " 'Beautiful,' just like it was my pet name for her, then I would see another part of her and move on to another pet name."

Maybe it was because Mr. Jefferson broke down like he did before me, that it allowed all the floodgates to open to the loving emotion he had for Joy. It seems that their feelings of love for each other had been bound together, so one part could not be separated from the other.

Everything was in perfect balance, and no one emotion would ever override the other for any length of time before it righted itself. Love and lust become one and the same. Both were in such perfect harmony that the vibrations were like that of the unearthly music that seemed to float in the air around them … It came up from the musty earth and down from the glorious heavens. They both believed that this was the spiritual aspect of their love, and along with all of the other parts, this was what God provided. It was another part of life and love that he gave to them, his children, for their happiness.

By the time my father finally stopped talking to me about the wonderful love life that he and his wife had had for each over, I knew that Paul Jefferson was telling the truth, and I had stopped hating my father. This left a space open inside me that was quickly filled with love for this man who was my dad and a far better man than any I had ever known, except for one other—the man who had raised me.

"I've had two good, loving men for my father, one black and one white, and I doubt if one in a thousand could say that and be telling the truth about himself. I have lots more folks to forgive now, too, and a great deal to learn about being a real man, like these two."

My old feeling of anger had completely left my soul, and I was a person free of what hatred could do to someone. Where should I begin? Right where I was, of course. Paul had other children, but I knew he liked me, and he had a wife who didn't seem to care too much about him. Maybe I was wrong because of the little while I'd been around her; just supper the few times she'd invited me to eat with them, but she sure acted like she wouldn't care if Paul lived or died. Made me wonder if my mother couldn't have taught her a thing or two about how to love a man and how to make him happy. It made my mother happy, too, 'cause Dad told me she was always going around singing and whistling those good gospel songs. Right then, I had the urge to go over and give my dad a big hug and ask him to forgive me for having such angry feelings toward him. I was so happy to have realized I was wrong about him.

"Well, son, we just about used up this whole night getting to know each other, and I'm glad you came over to tell me the story and let me know you were my son. So she named you Ezell. That sounds just like the kind of beautiful name Joy would have given you."

"Mr. Jefferson, first, is it alright if I call you Dad? And next, can I give you a big hug?"

"Sure you can, Ezell. Come on over here."

"Thanks, Dad. I missed you," I said, right in the middle of our big hug.

"And I missed you, too, Ezell. I hope to see a lot more of you now. Just think all of these years, and we didn't even get to know each other till now," said Paul.

"Hey, Dad, I know you and Mom were married 'cause I checked court records, but from all you told me, I was a first-class 'love child,' wasn't I?"

"Shore was, Ezee, still is. You are easy to love, that's for sure."

"That's what my best friend calls me, too, Dad! 'Ezee'! I always liked that name. Thanks."

"Is he the young man who knew how to fix those stirrups for the saddle his father made for me at Lenoir when we both lived there?"

"Surely is, Dad. He's my best friend, though most people don't know that. They think he picks on me, but he knows just how far I'll let him go before I come down on him. We have a little understanding about each other, and we both respect each other too. Billy hasn't received all the formal education I have, and it makes him seem different, but he's really not. He's smart as a whip and learns real fast, especially when he has to. So most folks are wrong about us. We had the same mother, you know."

"Didn't know that, son. How could that be?"

"I think I told you about the white man who found me and took me home with him. Well, he and his wife had a cook and housekeeper who had a son. In fact, about a month before I was born, and she nursed both Billy and me at the same time. For quite a few years, Billy was really jealous of me, but he finally grew out of it and we became good friends. He just doesn't know that yet. He's the only friend I have that's my age. Annie is still a little down on him for being so jealous of me. She thinks he was mean to me. She'll get over it as soon as she sees that Billy isn't like he used to be toward me. His jealousy has gone away, just like my anger toward you went away. Life is taking a turn-around for me, Dad. I'm so grateful I lived to see that day. It's really like a big kaleidoscope turning, you know?"

"How's that, son? What do you mean by 'a big kaleidoscope turning'?"

"I mean that now that I can see straight, I can see through it that our Creator made us all. Even though there are many colors and variations of colors, it is all good and beautiful. We really are all God's creatures, even to everything that has life, Dad. It's just that sometimes, the way we act causes other people to think God wouldn't have created that person. That's not true, is it? He just gave us freedom and a choice of how we act, and it's up to us to choose a way that pleases him and lets him know that we love him, or a way that makes him very sad for us and those we hurt."

"Gracious, son, but you think deeply and speak clearly. So, you have two mothers too? What's this woman's name?"

"Her name is Annie, and she's such a good and sweet woman. I love her, too, just like the other mother who saved my life by nursing me until she died, and because she put all of her clothes, coat, sweater, every-thing to try to keep me from freezing like she did. I'm sorry, Dad, I shouldn't have told you that, but you know her and how deep her love could be. You know she would lay down her life for either of us and that she would have done that for you too. So please don't hate me because of it, Dad."

"No, son, it's far too late for that. Now it only makes me treasure you more."

"Thank you, Dad … I was afraid to tell you why she froze—afraid you would hate me."

"I couldn't hate someone your mother loved so much, Ezell. It's what our Lord Jesus did for us all, and your mother believed in doing what he wanted us to do. Once, she told me that he had said that if we loved him, we would obey him and keep his commandments. This would be the way to prove our love for him, and not only through our prayers, reading the Bible, and doing good things."

"I'm glad you told me that, Dad. So she loved him, too, just like my other two mothers. Papa doesn't say as much about him, as Mama and Annie do. That may be because women seem better at talking about their feelings. What do you think, Dad?"

"Don't know, son. It could well be. I know I'm not so good at even knowing what I feel sometimes, how I feel, or if I feel. I didn't have that problem, though, when I was with Joy. I knew exactly how I felt about that woman—and other things too. She made me know just how good it was to even be alive. She was always singing songs about how beautiful life was and about loving others until they came to know God for themselves. Lots of those songs I can still remember, but I just can't sing them anymore. It's like she took them with her, but I know she wouldn't have done that. She would have left them for me. I still get a little confused about things."

"I'm sorry, Dad, and I hope the day comes when you can sing again. That will be a joy-filled day."

"Yes, it will, son … a joy-filled day. I want you to know you can stay with us for as long as you like—anytime. This is your home now, and we are your people. Your sisters and brothers are here, waiting to meet you tomorrow. So goodnight now, Ezell, my son. I'll see you in the morning."

"Good night, Dad … See you in the morning, and I'll take you up on that about staying with you some. I want to get to know you better and to know my brothers and sisters too. Thank you so much for wanting me to spend some time with all of you. I had hoped that we might hit it off."

"Of course, we'll hit it off! I want all of my children to get to know each other. I'll need to do a little talking this over with my woman, though. It'll be alright. You'll be most welcome here, Ezee …"

* * * * *

So, that's the story Ezell told me of how he came to find his real father.

Ezell spent time with his other family in West Point off and on for the next few years. He was happy with them, as well as with his family in

Prairie—Aunt Nettie, Uncle John, and me. This continued until America became involved in World War II and Ezell decided to join the military. He wanted to spend a few weeks with Uncle John, Aunt Nettie, Billy, Annie, and me before he left, in addition to wanting to get his adopted parents' approval for him to join the marines.

CHAPTER FOUR

I Thought, What Can I Be?

One day when Aunt Nettie was reminiscing about the time when Uncle John brought Ezell home as an infant, she told me that she knew the baby was going to need some milk or it would not make it through the winter. Fortunately, Annie, our cook, had recently given birth to her first child, a little boy by the name of Billy. Aunt Nettie had asked Annie if she would be willing to nurse Ezell too.

Annie quickly assured her. "Yes, ma'am, I's getting plenty of milk, and it is warm and rich. It'll do little Ezell a world of good, and Lord knows he needs it. If his mother hadn't given her life for his, he would of froze to death 'cause his pappy left home without laying in any firewood for the winter."

Aunt Nettie told me that she was ever so glad she had said yes to Annie's request—Annie had asked that her baby be allowed to stay in the kitchen of the big house so she could nurse him every few hours and because it was such a cold winter.

"She took quite a risk asking me that," Aunt Nettie said, "because none of the plantation homes, that I ever knew of, had a little colored baby living in the kitchen during the day. Annie must have sensed I was a little different from most plantation managers' wives," Aunt Nettie told me. "She was a brave young woman, as well as a good mother, cook, and housekeeper. Billy and Ezell were lucky little boys, and didn't even know it."

"Aunt Nettie, they were lucky to have you too. I know that I am, and I love you for being so good to all of us and especially to Uncle John."

"You probably know, dear, that I was a teacher before I met your Uncle John, and I only taught white children. Why, I never had my hand on a colored child until little Billy came to live in our kitchen."

"You did put your hand on little Billy, though, didn't you Aunt Nettie?"

"Why would you ever ask me such a question, Alva Jo?" she retorted.

"Because I know that you love children, and I know that you wanted a baby of your own, and Ezell and Billy are children and babies too. So just like you held and rocked Ezell, you touched and maybe even held Billy too. Did you, Aunt Nettie?"

"Well aren't you a smarty-pants?" she said. "If I had a little girl like you in my classroom, I would have boxed her jaws." Aunt Nettie sat quietly for a long while, and then in a much softer voice said, "Yes, Baby Girl, I did touch little Billy, and more than that, I lifted him up out of his cradle and held him in my arms. I just wanted to see what holding a little baby felt like, how it felt to have his tiny, little fingers curling around my thumb. He even smiled at me … His first smile, I think. Annie said she had never seen him smile, anyway. You must never tell your Uncle John this. I don't want him to know I did that. I don't even want Annie to know—or anyone else, for that matter. Can I trust you not to tell?"

"Oh yes, ma'am, and I am really good at being able to keep secrets. I promise you that I will never tell Uncle John, Annie, or anyone you even know. I love you, Aunt Nettie, and I know that you trust me. I won't let you down. I think you did a good thing. Aunt Myrtie told me that little babies that aren't held and touched will die. She said she read it in a medical book somewhere …"

It was only a few summers after Aunt Nettie confided in me that Annie did too. Often, Annie and I had time together while Aunt Nettie was teaching Ezell or she was reading and preparing to teach him. One day, Annie told me that Aunt Nettie used to have friends over to her home a long time ago, but they quit coming over to play bridge, and she and Uncle John quit going with them and their husbands to the horse shows in nearby West Point. Annie said these friends of theirs didn't like it that they adopted Ezell, not one little bit, and they never invited them to the parties or anything at their house ever again. Later, Aunt Nettie said that that was alright with her because with Ezell to bring up, she didn't have time for bridge, parties, and such. And that caring for Ezell was a lot more fun anyway. Uncle John thought they had never been good friends in the first place and that Aunt Nettie and he just found out in good time. "Who needs friends like that who don't stand by you when you decide how you want to live your life?" he said. "Not me!"

Annie and I were talking another day, and I noticed her eyes were all red, as if she had been crying.

"Have you been crying about something, Annie?" I asked.

"No, ma'am," she said and the next thing I knew, the truth was coming out. "Miss Alva Jo, I's been crying 'cause I hates it that I loves Ezell more than I loves Billy. Billy is my own, the baby I's give birth to, and I'm s'posed to love Billy more. I cries and cries about it, but my heart don't change. I gets so mad at Billy for the way he treats Ezell. He has hated Ezell from the very beginning.

"Miss Alva Jo, Ezell talked about a year before Billy did, 'cause Billy was so mad about his life after Ezell started nursing on me," Annie said. "Ezell's first big talking was 'Billy, he my bubba.' Billy's first words was 'Whup him, Mama, whup him!' Can you understand that, Miss Alva Jo? I swears it's de truth. He's always been doing bad things to Ezell. I knows when Ezell comes in with a bloody nose or a red eye that Billy done it. When I see Ezell and axed him what happened, he say something like, 'Oh, I jus' stepped on that ole rake, and it flew up and hit me,' or 'I got dis here when Big Ben up and accidentally kicked me.' I knows Ezell is more sure-footed than that, and he ain't truthing me. And when I goes home, there be Billy a-sitting and a-grinning like an ole possum with nary a scratch on him. I knows Ezell wouldn't touch a hair on his head. Pray to God to forgive me for wanting to hit Billy myself with my fist and that ole ball bat I keeps for protection. And I prays to God to forgive us both and to change Billy. Oh, what kind of mother am I to love somebody's child more than my own?"

"Annie, can I ask you a question? If it was Ezell doing that to Billy, which one would you be mad at and want to hit with your fist and the old bat?"

Annie almost shouted at me. "Miss Alva, you know which one. Ezell, of course!"

"I think that would be enough to make anyone very mad, Annie, and it's because you do love them both so much. Ezell once told me that we don't love one person more than another; we just love them differently. I love you, Annie, but right now, I need to go to my room and do some of my own thinking."

Both of these good women were suffering from a guilty conscious and, for the lack of the right person, talked to me—just a girl—about what was behind their suffering. This set me to thinking about what I wanted to do and be when I grew up. It started me to thinking about just how important trust and loyalty were, and that it was an honor to be trusted. It caused me to want to grow up wanting to be known as someone who could be trusted and who was good at listening. It also caused me to feel so good to be able to have helped those two women to choose for themselves what they wanted, and to stop thinking they had done something wrong, and to maybe even like themselves better.

Were there any jobs, I wondered, where someone could go to school or college to learn how, if needed, to help another person … like sometimes Ezell and Uncle John did for me?

CHAPTER FIVE

Basic Training for Ezell and Billy

Leaving for Camp Lejeune

*I*n the spring of 1942, Ezell was ready to board the train in Aberdeen for Montford Point, Camp Lejeune, North Carolina, where the new African-American marines were to receive their training. Uncle John, Aunt Nettie, and I went along, and Ezell brought Rose, who was his first real love, with him. Ezell had told me earlier that she was the most beautiful and sweetest woman that he had ever seen. She had big brown eyes, shiny dark hair, and a wonderful warm, outgoing personality.

It seems that early in World War II, the marines were the only branch of the military that accepted African-Americans. Later in the war, as the need for additional men became apparent, they were accepted in the army too. They were especially needed in the transportation area. Reading about the Red Ball Express, as well as the Tuskegee Airmen—one on the ground (truck drivers) and the other in the air (pilots)—was so interesting. Later still, they were used as pilots in smaller planes to escort, guard, and protect the large bombers. The Tuskegee Airmen were noted for their "zero score" of no bombers lost during combat missions.

Ezell bid us all goodbye and softly kissed Rose. I saw tears begin to form in his eyes, and he turned his face away and then quickly got on the train. It took Aunt Nettie only until the next day to declare that Rose was indeed a charming young lady and that she thought that Ezell had chosen wisely.

I just hoped that Rose would wait for Ezell and that Billy would stay out of Ezell's life. Aunt Nettie cried and cried. I cried too. I cried because I thought it was so sad that Ezell felt compelled to do this for a reason that, at age eleven, I didn't understand. Much later, when I was studying history about the various wars, I learned that so many people had lost their lives in World War II, and I still did not understand. Millions more were destroyed in other ways—still alive but with severe disabilities and pain that never would go away.

* * * * *

Ezell had just settled into his seat and pushed it back to get comfortable when he heard a "Pssspt!" behind him.

"Now, who would be trying to get my attention?" he thought. *I don't know anybody on this train so why the Pssspt!?*

Still thinking about the odd sound, Ezell said to himself, "There must be something wrong with the wiring that is making that noise. I'll just ignore it and hope that it is not a big problem." About that time, he felt a tug on his shirt.

I can't ignore that, he thought, so he turned slowly around to see who or what it was. "As I live and breathe! Billy, what the blazes are you doing here? I didn't see you anywhere at the station."

"That's 'cause I weren't out there. I wuz sitten here a-waiting for you." Billy had several belly laughs over this, until Ezell asked him to quieten down.

"Yes, sirree, sitten right here in this train car thinkin' bout how funny you wus gonna look when you seen me."

About that time, the train started up, and Billy and Ezell were on their way to their basic training camp. Except for a little time to sleep, they talked off and on for most of the trip. The closer Ezell and Billy got to Camp Lejeune, the more frightened they got, until Billy finally asked, "What they gonna do to us, Ezee?"

"Turn us into US Marines," replied Ezell.

"What do that mean, Ezee? How they gonna do that?"

"That means they are going to make men out of us and then send us overseas to where they need us to fight the Japs. Yes, we're going to learn to fight now, to kill people, not just to give them a bloody nose."

Ezell had been told this by a marine recruiter, and he didn't know that the African-Americans didn't get to fight for the first several years but were used mainly as support personnel.

"But, Ezee, I don't know if I wants to do dat. Don't that mean those Japs is gonna be trying to do the same thing to me too?"

"Yes, Billy, it does. Thousands of them are being taught right now to kill us and to hate us just as much as we hate them. Then, when it's all over and half a million or so people all over the world get killed, the war will stop. And of the people who are left, they will sign a peace treaty and then go back to talking nice to each other again like nothing even happened."

"Do that mean like it was in school—when the fightin' is over, we all go back to being friends again?"

"Something like that, Billy, but not quite, 'cause a lot of us are going to be dead and buried before that happens."

"How long is all this going to take? Do you think me and you are gonna be dead before it stops? I sure don't want to get killed, and I don't even want you to either, Ezee. Sometimes I almost hated you, but now, with thinking about death, I don't hate you at all."

"Then we will have to learn how to kill first, and try to save each other. Won't we, Billy?"

"Ezee, I don't want to think about this no mo'. Why did we ever talk about it anyway?"

"Because we have to know things now so we won't get killed. Okay, Billy?"

"Guess so, Ezee … Oh, Lordy, Lordy, maybe I never should have signed up for this."

"Too late now, Billy. Just make up your mind to do the best you can, and you will be just fine."

After a few more hours of riding the rails, talking back and forth, and snoozing a bit, Ezell and Billy and the rest of the recruits arrived at the train station where there was a bus waiting to take them to Camp Lejeune. Upon arriving, they were met by a short, mean-looking, grumpy sergeant whose name was Rottweiler. He lost no time snarling at them to "Fall in!" for their first haircut.

"Billy, don't say a word about it when they do it, because we are going to be sheared like sheep," Ezell said.

"How you know 'bout this, Ezee?" asked Billy.

"I know because I read some papers the military mailed me before I left home about what things were going to be like here. I'll try to help you if you will just listen and do what I tell you," Ezell replied.

"Okay, Ezee, thanks."

"Now, after our hair has been cut, we will all get in a line and go get the clothes we will be wearing from now on. You'll just need to tell them what size you wear, after they ask you what size."

"Okay, thanks."

"Why are you doing all this 'thanks' stuff, Billy? Ain't never heard you be that nice before."

"'Cause I'm scared, bad scared, Ezee. Those big ole ugly, mean white boys scare the daylights outta me."

"Wait till you see those ugly little slant-eyed yellow boys with rifles in their hands," Ezell said.

"All right, you two scumbags!" shouted Sergeant Rottweiler. "Stop that talking, and line up to get your hair cut. Then get your uniforms. You act like two little girls. You aren't in no beauty shop or ladies' clothing store, either, and nobody wants to hear two sissies talking." Sergeant Rottweiler got within two inches of Billy's face and shouted at him again, "Get your shoes, uniforms, and other crap, and get lined up!"

"Yes, sir!" both Billy and Ezell said simultaneously.

"Put your clothes in the barracks, and then fall in for your shots. When you come back, Drill Sergeant Verbie will talk to you about your daily training routines, briefings, physical training, drills, and ceremonies," said Sergeant Rottweiler.

* * * * *

"Lordy me, I thought Sergeant Verbie would never stop talking," said Billy. "And then he said our day starts at 0500, which I think is five in the morning."

"That's right, and you better learn all the military time, too, Billy."

"So at 0500, we're s'posed to make our beds, straighten up around here, brush our teeth, shave, and some more stuff."

"We meet with the rest of our squad and divide the cleaning and other jobs we're supposed to do. Then, after going out the door with our rifle in our hands, we are supposed to get into formation," said Ezell.

"Then what happens?" asked Billy.

"We stand at attention while the sergeant calls the roll, and then our platoon will march out for our morning calisthenics. After that, we go back to the barracks, shower, and change into our uniforms. Billy, we need to be sure and straighten the barracks up again, or they will get us for that. Remember all of this; I may not be able to tell you again."

"Alright, but I'm really hungry now, so I wonder when we'll eat."

"Right after we get back into formation and march to the mess hall, we will have to get through eating as fast as we can and then get outside. There'll be a lot of others waiting to sit down and eat. After we finish eating, we'll march again. Then Sergeant Verbie will brief us on the rest of the day's activities. I wish you had gotten those papers they sent me, and you would know a lot of these things, too, Billy. Next, it will be back to the barracks, where someone will teach us about military time and how to hang our clothes, arrange our foot lockers, and clean the latrine."

About that time, the drill sergeant walked over and started talking to the squad about what things he expected them to learn and become proficient in doing. The following summarized what he discussed:

1.   Through training, you are taught many basic combat skills such as use of the hand grenade, the field environment, and rifle marksmanship.

2.   Our training teaches men how to be combat specialists, including intelligence, medical, supply, and transportation support, and military occupational and specialists.

3.   In basic training, you also experience intense competition between different companies such as marksmanship and bayonet practice, hand-to-hand combat, and obstacle courses. This is done to see which company gets the largest number of "winner" flags. The activities are extremely competitive.

4.   In addition, marines are prepared for the rigors of night infiltration. To graduate from basic training, you must complete all training events during the nine weeks. Competencies included qualification with the M-

16 rifle, the physical fitness test, qualifying with hand grenades, and the ability to pass the "End of Cycle" test.

Just before lights out that night, Ezell wrote Rose a short, quick letter.

June 12, 1942
My dearest Rose,

It's only been a few days since I said goodbye to you in Aberdeen, but it seems like two months to me. Being away from you, though, caused me to know more than ever just how fortunate I am to have found you. You really are the sweetest, kindest person that I have ever known, and I am so looking forward to being with you again.

Take good care of yourself and stay safe until I return to take care of you for the rest of our lives.
P.S. Billy is here with me, and I am writing to let Annie know so she will not worry about where he went.

Yours always,
Ezell

In a few days, Ezell had time to write to Rose again.

Dearest Rose,

We just finished another day at the camp. It really wasn't all that bad, but a few of the men did pass out during the physical training session. Billy and I, as you might have guessed, were not among them.

Rose, you are always on my mind. Sometimes I tell myself, "Rose is waiting for me," and because of that, I should do my very best. I know you are going to be proud of me for doing this well. Because of that, my dear Rose, nothing is too hard for me to do.

At the end of this nine-week training program, on August 10, we can invite our family and friends here to see us graduate. I would like for you to come down with Mama and Papa Oldham. Would you please do this, dear Rose?

My love,

Ezell

P.S. This is a copy of our daily schedule, which was just put up. I wanted you to have it so you would know what I was doing any time that you might think of me.

Daily Training Schedule

5:00 a.m. – Wake up

5:30 a.m. – Physical Training

6:30 a.m. – Breakfast

8:30 a.m. – Training

12:00 p.m. – Lunch

1:00 p.m. – Training

5:00 p.m. – Dinner

6:00 p.m. – Drill Sergeant Time

8:30 p.m. – Personal Time

9:30 p.m. – Lights Out

Love and kisses,

Ezell

On August 9, 1942, not knowing that Billy's mother was coming for graduation the next day, Ezell was anxiously awaiting the arrival of his family and his girlfriend. Billy had made it through all of the nine weeks of basic training, too, but he was back in the barracks thinking that no one cared whether he graduated or not. Although Ezell felt bad about Billy being so depressed, he decided there was very little that he could do about it, and he told himself that he wasn't going to let it get him down too. After all, he would soon be seeing Rose again, and he had every intention of persuading her to marry him before he left to go overseas. As he set about wondering if this was the right thing to do, a little blue Ford came up to the gate packed with Papa and Mama, Billy's mother, Annie, Rose, and, of course, myself.

Glory be, Annie came, too! Ezell thought. *If I run like crazy, I can tell Billy to come out here, and I can still get back to the parking area by the time they'll be getting out of the car.*

"Billy! Billy! Get yourself out here on the double. The sweetest woman you know is here to see you, so come on. Yell, Billy, so I will know that you heard me!" shouted Ezell.

Billy yelled, "Okay, Ezee, I'm coming just as soon as I put my shoes back on! Where do I go?"

"The parking area!" Ezell shouted back.

By the time Uncle John had found his way around and stopped, both Ezell and Billy were standing there, wearing their nicely pressed uniforms and newly polished shoes. They were waiting for Rose, Annie, and the rest of their family members to see them.

Everyone was overjoyed and ever so proud of their two men, who were now full-fledged United States Marines. There was great laughing and talking and a few tears of happiness shed, as well as some hugging and kissing. Only Rose purposely hung back some from the emotional demonstrations. Ezell had already told us that she was a little reserved and quite lady-like—whatever that meant. I was glad to see Ezell so happy and so confident. Even Billy seemed to be more sure of himself and less inclined to be shy around Uncle John and Aunt Nettie. Billy and Annie were filled with happiness, seeing, admiring, and hugging each other once more. I couldn't help but laugh when I thought of the times long ago when Annie thought she couldn't love Billy as much as she loved Ezell. The thought gave me a good excuse to have fun and laugh very loudly, just like everyone else was doing.

The next day, August 10, the battalion commander met with the families and friends and discussed combat training and experiences and answered questions. We also met the drill sergeant and observed more of the maneuvers and mock battles until it was time to leave.

Ezell and Billy were pleased to receive two weeks' leave, and consequently returned with their families in an extremely overcrowded car. In fact, it was so miserably overcrowded that Billy and Ezell found some boards, tied them together, and proceeded to tie themselves on top of the car, and home we went.

CHAPTER SIX

Romance—Ezell and Rose

*B*oth men enjoyed being back in Prairie. Ezell said he enjoyed working alongside Uncle John-his Papa. But I think he did it to keep busy and to keep his mind off the fact that Rose couldn't be with him at this time because she was working on a research project. On both weekends, Ezell did make the trip to the nearby college town to be with Rose. Fortunately, he said he understood just how important going to college was and that keeping her grades up was important to him, also.

Rose had seen how her mother had physically suffered and knew how poor they all were. To survive, her mother had had to depend on the generosity of the current male in her life. After seeing the men coming and going in her house, Rose had vowed to herself that she would develop some skill so she would never have to depend on someone else for economic well-being. Before she was thirteen, Rose had a goal of getting a college degree, and now she was well on her way to doing just that. "No man is going to stop me, either," declared Rose. "Nor is any man going to assist me in getting my degree, because I don't want to be obligated to anyone," Rose told her friends—including me, but not Ezell.

Rose showed me her diary one day. In it she wrote, "If I ever do marry, it will be for love and not for need. I have to be able to take care of myself before I ever think about marriage. I know that Ezell wants to marry me, but I'm just not ready to take that step at this time. I believe he does understand a little, but he has never had to live as I did. He is so good to me, though, and I can see the way his eyes light up every time I walk through the door. I think he does love me, but he is going to have to wait until I am ready—if I ever am! Better stop all this writing and get myself over to the library to use the microfiche machine and look up a few more things for Professor Martin. He said he wanted what I had researched by this Friday. I'm so glad that I got this job for the summer, even if it is for only twenty hours per week. The pay, $400 a month, will help, and all of my books are free because most of them are shelved here where I work, and the rest of them are in the library. Ezell will be off on Saturday, and I promised him some time during the day and a movie that night. I'm looking forward to being with him, but I'll need to watch that I don't spend too many hours away from my job and my schoolwork."

Rose continued to write in her diary every day. Sometimes, she'd let me read it. She was worried, like the time she wrote, "If we go to the 6:30 movie, that gives us two hours, so we'll have a few minutes to talk, have a sandwich, and be with each other awhile before the dorm doors are locked at 10 p.m. That's good, because I don't want to toss a pebble against an upstairs window. I've had plenty tossed at mine … It's a good thing our dorm mother is almost deaf, or she would hear that big door swinging open. There are only about thirty-five girls in this big ole building during the summer months and even less, they tell me, during the fall and winter semesters. Just maybe I'll be able to go to college during those semesters before too long. Maybe I could really save my money, get a scholarship, and work on campus. If I do everything in my power, I think there would be a way to make it happen! It's almost 9:30 now, and I have all the numbers Professor Martin said he needed to work on this weekend regarding the effects of three different types of cow feed on milk production, so I'll head back to the dorm and get the clothes I have on now washed and ironed for tomorrow, get my bath, and go to bed …"

* * * * *

As soon as Ezell arrived at the campus, he called the telephone number Rose had given him and asked the person who answered to please get Rose. She lived on the third floor, and it took quite awhile for her to get down the stairs to the first floor where the only phone in the building was located. That's just the way things were in the girls' dorm in the 1940s. By the time Rose got to the phone, she was out of breath, and her heart was pounding for more than just one reason. Rose told herself, however, that her heart was beating faster just because she had run down three flights of stairs. When Ezell heard her breathing heavily, he asked what was wrong, so she went through the entire "running down the stairs" explanation for his benefit.

Ezell's first question was "How soon can I see you, and will you go to lunch with me?"

Rose answered, "Yes, I can go to lunch with you."

"What time will you be ready?" Ezell asked.

"Give me thirty minutes," Rose replied. She had already laid out her newly washed, starched, and ironed dress, along with her best shoes, clean socks, undies, and a pretty new hair ribbon. Oh, how she wanted to look pretty for Ezell, hoping that his eyes would light up like they always did when he saw her.

When she came down the stairs he said, "Rose, you've got to be the most gorgeous creature that ever set foot on this Earth."

Rose replied, "Oh, you know there's a lot of girls here that are prettier than I am."

"Then I don't want to see them, because they wouldn't be real," retorted Ezell.

"What do you mean by that, Ezell? You're not making sense."

"You know the story of the Velveteen Rabbit, don't you? Didn't your mother read it to you when you were a little girl?"

"Ezell, my mother couldn't read, and she wouldn't have had the time if she could have. She had a baby nearly every year for so many years that I can't count. Since I was the oldest, I had to help her deliver and bury them. Some lived, and some died. We buried them in the back yard."

"Oh, my darling Rose, I didn't know. Please forgive me."

"There's a whole lot you don't know about me, Ezell, and it is alright. How could you know? Let's just say that now it is what makes me so determined to raise myself up and out of my family and be a financially independent woman."

"Wow, I didn't realize you felt like that."

"Does it bother you to know it?"

"No, my dear, it does not. It just lets me know that you are trusting enough to tell me exactly who you are and what your dreams are. I always knew that you were not an ordinary girl, and I admire you for it."

Rose and Ezell enjoyed their lunch in the picturesque cafeteria and then walked around the campus. Rose showed Ezell some of her favorite buildings and places on campus. Later, Ezell found a book that was interesting, so he began reading it while sitting beside Rose as she was finishing her work for the first day. Rose had a few more hours of work left for the next day, reading from old newspapers and microfiche. While Rose was doing this, Ezell finished his book and then went for a run before it was time to meet her again.

It was getting close to five o'clock before Rose and Ezell went to the grill for a sandwich and Coke. As Ezell pulled a chair out for Rose, he asked Rose if she had received his letters.

"Yes, I did, and they were so informative and well-written."

Ezell was disappointed, and then he asked her, "Could you tell from the way I wrote that I was deeply in love with you?"

"Well, are you?" asked Rose.

Not to be deterred, Ezell continued, "I'm senselessly and stupidly in love with you!"

"Why do you say it like that, Ezell?" asked Rose.

"Because my mind isn't mine anymore. When I'm working or learning something new, my thoughts are of you. So sometimes, I make a mess of what I'm doing. I've never been that way before in my life, and it started right after I met you."

There was no one else at the grill on that particular Saturday evening, so they could talk freely. Ezell continued, as he gazed into Rose's eyes: "You are everything I have ever dreamed, hoped, or longed for in a woman. I want to marry you before I go overseas. I want you to be my wife and to wait for me to come home to you. Then, when I do come back, it will be to our home and our love. And if I don't come back, you would be entitled to some monetary benefits because you were my wife. Maybe it might be enough to send you on through college without you having to work so hard, like you do now. What do you say, Rose?"

Rose began to cry. Big tears began to roll down her cheeks, and she said, "Ezell, I do love you, but I made a vow to myself a long time ago that I would finish college before I ever married, and I must stick to that vow. Oh, I hope that you will understand that it is my one goal in life; it's been what's kept me through my young life and teen years. When things were so bad at home, it kept me on track and studying, even when I was so hungry that I would dream about eating and then wake up chewing my tongue. That vow was made by me to myself; if I can't keep that one, then I can't keep any other. Do you understand, dear, sweet Ezell?"

"Yes, I do. And I'll wait for you. Will you wait for me?" Ezell asked.

"Of course I will. I've never laid eyes on another man since I met you. I've even said to myself, 'That man is going to be the father of my children one day,' " Rose replied.

"Did you honestly mean that, Rose?" asked Ezell. "I've had the exact same thought."

"My dear Ezell, if we are going to be on time for that movie, we are going to have to leave now," said Rose.

The two of them started walking hand-in-hand down the sidewalk, past the creamery, then past the railroad tracks toward town. The town was almost in sight as they continued to walk. The first thing that caught their attention was the brightly colored lights of the town's Ritz Theater. Upon their arrival, Ezell stepped up and bought their tickets, and they went inside to take their seats. About that time, the newsreel started, and one of the features shown that evening was the sinister, smiling face of a Japanese soldier with fanged teeth with the announcer saying, "Ladies and gentlemen, this is the monster your sons and husbands are fighting overseas. This man is faking a smile, because no one that evil smiles. This kind of man is a baby-eating monster. Buy more Victory Bonds and support your sons and husbands, who are fighting to save your lives and your children's lives against the Japs who want to conquer America."

The movie started, and Ezell and Rose sat back comfortably to enjoy it. That evening, they watched a rerun of a movie that came out in 1936 called *The Trail of the Lonesome Pines*. According to Rose, it was based on a romance novel of the same name. And it was the first full-length film to be shot outdoors and only the second one to be shot in Technicolor.

As they were walking back to the campus, Ezell asked, "Did you read the book, as well, Rose?"

"Yes," she replied, "and I felt that the movie followed the book very well."

"What about that other Technicolor movie, *The Wizard of Oz*? I thought it was good one too."

"Yes, it was, but this one is a romance movie," Rose replied. "Speaking of romance, look, look, Ezell! There's a full moon out tonight!"

They both stopped talking and gazed at the moon for a while.

"Rose, I'll never see a full moon for the rest of my life without thinking of you," said Ezell.

"Nor will I," said Rose. "This evening has been wonderful, my love, but I must go now to get back to the dorm before the door is locked."

Each looked forward to their next weekend together and said their goodbyes with a passionate kiss and a fond embrace. Little did they know it was to be their last night together for three long years.

When Ezell returned to the plantation in Prairie, a telegram from the war department was awaiting him. He nervously opened the yellow envelope and was astonished at what he read: "You are directed to report for active duty at Camp Lejeune, Montford, North Carolina, by 1800 hours, August 20, 1942." He repeated the words aloud for Uncle John and Aunt Nettie, and both were visibly upset. They hugged Ezell for a while, and then Aunt Nettie rushed upstairs, sobbing all the way. Sleep would elude her that night.

"Son, you had better get your things together so we can leave for the bus station in the morning," said Uncle John. He said little more, and it was clear that he had a lump in his throat and was having trouble talking.

"What should I say to Rose?" asked Ezell.

"You have a lot to do before sundown, so it would be best for you to call her after you get through. I believe she will have heard about it long before you call, but call her as soon as you can, and tell her goodbye and how much you love her," said Uncle John.

The telegram Ezell and many other servicemen received was part of a large-scale emergency call-up caused by an American defeat in the

Pacific. It meant that America had to immediately bring all of its available manpower to fight the Japanese. Despite a valiant, month-long defense against an overwhelming number of Japanese forces by the American and Filipinos, the island of Bataan had fallen. The surviving defenders, 12,000 US soldiers and 64,000 Filipino soldiers, had then been forced to march day and night to a Filipino prison camp. They had been treated inhumanely, and along the way many had died from exhaustion, starvation, or from being shot, bayoneted, or beheaded ...

The next morning, Uncle John, Aunt Nettie, Ezell, and I were up early. Aunt Nettie had already told Annie that she wanted to cook breakfast; she wanted her "baby" to remember that he has a loving mother who enjoyed cooking for him and a home to come back to when he returned.

After Ezell had talked with Rose, he called Billy to find out if he had received a letter too. Billy had, and was feeling somewhat alarmed. They both made plans for going to camp and to arrive there by the next day. Camouflaged army trucks were already there to take the men to the port where they would board a Liberty ship bound for the South Pacific: American Samoa, to be specific. The ships left port on August 22, 1942. An aircraft carrier and numerous destroyer escorts pulled out for Guadalcanal right as Ezell and Billy's ship did.

CHAPTER SEVEN

Jungle Warfare Training

$\mathcal{T}$ he trip over was long and surprisingly uneventful. Occasionally, Billy and Ezell would find time to stand out on the deck and talk. Most of the time, their conversation referred back to the people they loved the most: Uncle John, Aunt Nettie, Annie, Rose, and me. Ezell even carried a picture of Rose in his billfold. One day after talking for a while about all of us, Ezell and Billy started talking about the ocean beneath them. It seemed that both Ezell and Billy liked to watch the movements of the water and the choppy waves, with their white foam. Sometimes, they would even see large fish, whales, and such swimming around underneath them. The moon was shining brightly with night, which of course reminded Ezell of Rose.

"Billy, why don't you go down below and get some sleep? I'll be there soon, I've got some thinking about my Rose to do."

"Sure, Ezee, I understand. Good night."

"Good night, Billy."

Ezell sat down and began thinking about Rose and found himself saying half aloud, "Oh, my darling Rose. How I miss you. I miss seeing you, touching you, holding you in my arms, and kissing you. I pray that I will be allowed to be with you again and that I will be able to return to you. May God bless and protect you tonight and every night that I am away."

Rose, back home in Crawford, Mississippi, was writing a letter to Ezell that very night.

August 29, 1942
My darling,

How I wish you were here now, because it is such a beautiful night with a big, bright moon in the sky. The night winds have cooled the day's heat down for a while, and I can feel the evening breeze and hear the whip-poor-wills calling. You remember how it was on those warm Mississippi nights, my love? I am sitting in my little bedroom at home with the windows pushed up all the way and thinking of you. Oh, how much I love and miss you. Except for your absence, my life has been much, much happier since I started college. But ever much more so since I met you. Please take good care of yourself and write as soon as you can.

Love,

Rose

Ezell was another week closer to the Jungle Warfare Training Camp in Tutulia, American Samoa, when he received the dainty white envelope from Crawford, Mississippi. He was overjoyed. It was from Rose. At first, he read over the entire page as fast as he could. Then he reread it very slowly so he could savor every word. As he carefully folded the envelope and placed it in his breast pocket, there were tears in his eyes. Afterward, when he went below to sleep, he caught himself saying, "Dear, sweet Rose. Thank you for the beautiful letter."

Later, Ezell would give this account of Guadalcanal in his letters home: "My next day was spent very much the same as the previous days—getting up at 0600, grooming and dressing, reporting on deck for exercise, and then reporting to the galley for breakfast. After breakfast, the command divided the men into two groups because the lecture room could only accommodate a limited number of men. The first group received information from the battlefield and reviewed strategies and the reasons for making changes. The other group spent their time cleaning weapons to ensure they operated properly in battle. The next day, the two groups would be switched. On other days, the number and size of the groups would vary depending on the activity.

"From midafternoon onward to the evening meal was downtime on the ship for the soldiers going to the Pacific. It was a time to talk with the chaplain, pray, write letters home, wash clothes, go up on the deck to get some fresh air, read, and talk with each other. Some of the men played cards, told stories and jokes, and spoke of what was ahead for them. All were afraid, with some becoming quite nervous, which resulted in a loss of appetite and insomnia."

Later in the day, the sergeant talked with the men about their jungle warfare training in American Samoa. The training was to be done in extremely high heat and humidity. Numerous large insects lived in the tropics, coupled with mosquitoes bearing dengue fever and malaria. Centipedes as long as six inches, with poisonous claws or fangs, were just some of the other pests. A microscopic worm that was more dangerous than a centipede was a parasite also spread by the mosquito. This thread-like worm lived only in the human lymph system. Their disease, called lymphatic filariasis, had been known to infect millions of people in the tropics and subtropic areas of the world.

For the next weeks before arriving in American Samoa, most of the soldiers talked mainly about jungle warfare and how the marine camp there would be different from the boot camp experience at Montford Point. Most of the soldiers thought that if they could survive boot camp for nine weeks in the heat of midsummer in North Carolina, they could survive in American Samoa, or Tutuila, for three weeks—ugly worms and mosquitos, or not. Besides, they were looking forward to getting their "land legs" back again.

Learning firsthand about the brutality of the enemy and things like the Bataan Death March would come later, after their arrival on Guadal-canal. They would hear it from the battle-seasoned soldiers, who had seen it with their own eyes.

Right now, they were looking forward to getting out of the confine-ment of the ship, which was packed should-to-shoulder with men.

Finally, the day came when the men saw their ship was maneuver-ing to enter the naturally created harbor in Pago Pago, the capital of American Samoa. Although the island was only 13 miles long and 4 miles wide, the harbor was large enough for one of America's largest ships, so there was little trouble getting the Liberty ship in and docked.

The soldiers were on land again, and what a beautiful piece of land it was. The sky was a clear azure blue that almost looked like a painting; the landscape was full of the brightest colors imaginable. Palm trees were

Harbor in American Samoa

a lush green, and there was hardly a square inch of soil around them and outward that wasn't covered with vegetation. The mountains were once dormant volcanoes that were currently covered with emerald-colored moss and other young green plants and trees that gently swayed in the breeze. Most of the soldiers had sore necks the next few days from looking at the volcanic mountains, the vastness of the ocean, the colorful plants and animals, and especially the indigenous people.

A greeting party of Samoans met the big ship as it entered the harbor. Included were the mayor and his wife and the local high school band, which played native Samoan music. The young people had brought small versions of steel drums, banjo-like instruments, and maracas. They played one song after another, each one sounding louder and more joyful than the one before. Typical of the Samoan people were their broad smiles, their movements to the rhythm of the music, and brightly colored sarongs known as lava-lavas.

The Samoans presented large, fragrant fresh flowers to the guests. The rhythm of the music, the swaying young people, the heavenly fragrances, and the colorful clothing was almost overwhelming to the soldiers. The welcoming smiles and mist from the sea, combined with a pleasant breeze and warm sunshine was also mesmerizing to the marines and soldiers. The young American soldiers viewed the island much as the natives did and referred to it as "paradise."

As a gloriously colorful sunset appeared on the ocean that evening, the mayor invited the ship's crew to stay for the Samoan delicacy of day-long roasted pig tied in coconut-water-soaked banana leaves. On their plates were baked bananas, rice, turkey tail, and a light, fluffy coconut dessert that resembled cotton candy. Conversation between the natives and the soldiers was very easy because a majority of the Polynesians spoke English, as well as their native language. English was taught in the schools of American Samoa.

The next morning after refueling, the ship departed for the nearby island of Tutuila, which was 4 miles offshore from American Samoa. It was where the marines and soldiers were to receive their jungle warfare training. Two weeks of the training went by rapidly. Reports came into the camp daily from Guadalcanal regarding the conditions there. Of course, this was the major topic of discussion, regarding coming face-to-face with the "Japs."

Just as the troops had started their third week of training, they received the news that Washington had learned that the Japanese were building a runway and an air base on one of the Solomon Islands. This, of course, was Guadalcanal. To make matters worse, the runway location would be close enough to bomb Australia. Before the airway was finished, the marines needed to take the island back. Everyone was then ordered to board the ship that was waiting for them in the Pago Pago harbor headed for Guadalcanal.

CHAPTER EIGHT

War in the South Pacific

*E*zell wrote several informative letters home to Uncle John, Aunt Nettie and Rose. Afterward, he wrote personal love letters to Rose. None of those to her were ever recovered.

August 27, 1942
Somewhere in the Pacific Ocean

Dear Mama, Papa, and Rose,

On August 6, we stood on the deck of our ship at Guadalcanal and watched as the group of ships fired their cannons and the planes above us dropped bombs. The noise was terrible. Breakfast was early that morning at 0500 and consisted of steak and eggs. Even with this kind of good food, it was hard to eat. After breakfast, we were ordered to get ready to disembark.

Going down the sides of the ship, there were mishaps and a few fatal accidents. This didn't help our morale, and the bombing was almost deafening. For the marines who had headed to American Samoa for training, the war was on.

High waves caused the landing craft to rise and fall 5 to 10 feet each time they passed, and the constantly changing height difference was very dangerous. Several of the soldiers were severely injured trying to board, and two were crushed to death between the ship and the landing craft. Regardless of the immediate danger, we had to depart as soon as everyone was inside.

The landing craft's propulsion engines were going at full throttle, and the noise was almost deafening as it fought each wave to get to the beach. We were tossed about so much that I was afraid we would capsize and drown. None of us could swim with a 65–70 pound backpack full of bullets.

When we finally hit the beach, the front door of the landing craft dropped down into the water, and we fully expected the Japs to fire upon us as soon as it did; but nothing happened. We jumped into the waist-high water and waded ashore as quickly as we could and took what little cover there was. The landing craft, now much lighter, reversed its engines and headed back to the ship for another load of soldiers.

The welcoming silence was in sharp contrast to all of the noise that we had been exposed to during the last few minutes. The beach seemed almost surreal and moving in slow motion. However, it was just my imagination. Although the Japs didn't attack us on the beach, we were sure they were close by and probably hiding somewhere in the hills. It was our job to go and get them, and I knew that I would be ready to fight whenever the time came. I really wanted to see what the Japs looked like, because I had never seen one before.

Our first day on the island was spent going through the jungle to get to a hill known as Grassy Knoll. Unfortunately, our maps were obsolete and had the names of hills and rivers all mixed up. Particularly oppressive was the heat and humidity. It was much worse than in American Samoa, because cool ocean breezes could not penetrate the thick foliage. We were exhausted before we were even halfway up the hill. Sergeant Odom halted our approach and told us to dig and get in a fox-hole. He ordered us to shut up about the heat and humidity, to eat our rations, and then go to sleep. We did, but it was very difficult because mosquitoes were biting us all the time. Each of us was limited to only one canteen of water, and there was precious little water left to digest our dried food and crackers.

At sunrise, we were ordered to march back to the beach and set up defenses against any Japs that might try to land and come up behind us. Just about the time we got back to the beach, several Jap torpedo bombers flew over us so low that we could see the red "meatball" insignia clearly on their wings. I could even see the pilots, who turned their heads and looked at us. Sometimes, they were grinning. The pilots were not interested in the few of us on the beach; they were after the ships. One of them came in low, heading straight toward the

USS Ambassador, the Liberty ship that brought us over. The plane dropped its torpedo and then banked sharply to the left to avoid being hit by flying debris from the expected explosion. Our hearts sank as we saw and heard the result. We watched our supply ship slip beneath the waves. Four cruisers suffered the same fate during the night, and the next morning we christened the area "Iron Bottom Bay."

With no way to get home and only half of our supplies unloaded, we were left with only two options—take the island or die trying. Neither Billy nor I had guns until our ship sank. We were just "support personnel" because we were African-Americans. This was when our sergeant threw two guns at us and told us we were "fighting men" now.

We were alone, and the only food we had was that which we carried on our backs. A search party was sent out to find more, but all they could locate were some stores of rice and oats that had been left behind by the Korean construction workers. The rice and oats were infested with maggots. However, we found that if you dumped the rice and oats into water, most of the bugs floated to the top and could be scooped out. It still took a strong stomach to eat what was left, but after a while, we considered the maggots and bugs to be just "meat." Before long, everybody was sick.

Two months before we landed, an American pilot had flown over the island and observed what appeared to be a small clearing in the jungle. He had concluded that it was an airstrip in the early stages of construction and had reported that fact. The information had soon reached the Joint Chiefs of Staff in Washington, D.C., where it immediately rose to "monumental" importance. It seems the strip was close enough to be used to bomb Australia and could also be used as a marshaling point for additional Pacific Island conquests. As such, we were given the job to secure the inoperable "airstrip" on Guadalcanal and did so. However, we paid dearly for the victory. Five days later, military engineers, who were commonly known as the Seabees in the Pacific, worked from dawn to dusk and completed an operable landing strip. We were very proud when the first of our fighter planes and big bombers landed safely on the island. It was one step closer to ending the War.

The first real fight on the land of the island began at 0130 hours on August 21. It was called the Battle of Tenaru River. The Japs had come marching across the beach, and when they reached the river, they spread out and formed a single line. At first, only one or two rifle shots were fired by our defense positions near the river. But when a line of fire came from their right end, we knew they were attacking in earnest. The rifle firing increased, and then some of our machine guns joined in. Lt. Reeves called for more machine guns to be placed into action, but we only had four because all the rest had gone down with the supply ship. Fortunately for us, they were at the exact spot where the Japs decided to cross the river. Why they chose that particular crossing is a mystery, because the river was deeper in some places than others, and they were not tall, and many drowned. The rest of the enemy found themselves in neck-deep water without the ability to use their guns.

The next thing I knew, all hell broke loose. Suddenly, the darkness became as bright as day with barrel flashes from all of the shooting. The river seemed to be filled with enemy helmeted heads, with all of them moving in our direction. They were determined and kept coming, even though we relentlessly fired upon them time and time again. There were many to be dealt with, and our rifle barrels soon became too hot to touch. Some of the Japs succeeded in crossing the river and reaching our two-man foxhole-defense position. There, they found a few of our men so tired and exhausted that they had fallen into a deep sleep. One Jap officer jumped into a foxhole and viciously hacked up two solders with his sword before one of our boys shot him. We kept firing until there was no one left to shoot. After that, the only night sounds came from the wounded and the dying. It was horrible!

During the night, we took turns manning the defense perimeter. It was spooky business because everything was so black and the jungle was so thick. All kinds of noises could be heard out there, and we could never tell if it was an iguana or a Jap soldier sneaking up on us. Every time someone fired at a sound, the whole defense line would open up, and it sounded like a battle was being fought. Switching off every two hours with the guy in the same foxhole did not give either much sleep.

In the morning, we found that the river had risen considerably, even though there had not been any rain. It was caused by the bodies of Japanese soldiers, which had washed downstream and formed a dam. The subsequent flooding created a pile of corpses about 5 feet high. Our chaplain had the unpleasant duty of removing dog tags from about forty of our fallen comrades and then giving each an identification label. All of our dead were subsequently buried in a small cemetery near what was to become known as Henderson Field. That cemetery continued to grow in size as the war progressed, and ultimately became the largest American cemetery on any of the Pacific Islands.

We heard stories about the Bataan Death March, where Allied soldiers were bayoneted indiscriminately when they fell on the ground from hunger and exhaustion. As a result, our hatred of the Japs grew daily, and as far as I know, we never took a prisoner afterward. It was clear we were fighting a brutal enemy that totally ignored the Geneva Convention.

Last night was terrible, Papa, and I'm glad it is over. I don't feel good about having to kill a man, even if he has killed lots of ours. We sunk to their level so fast that I'm sometimes ashamed of being part of the human race. The only thing I feel good about, darling Rose, is that I know now that I've seen the enemy at their worst and that we were able to defeat them.

I will write every chance I get. It took me almost three weeks to get this letter written because I could only write during daylight and when no bullets were flying.

Love to all,

Ezell

January 5, 1943

Dear Papa, Mama, and Rose,

A great day has at long last arrived. We are being replaced with a fresh supply of troops from America!

After five months of fighting, we won over fifty land campaigns, and Australia is no longer in danger of being bombed. Even better though, especially for many of the men who might have died here, we were sent to Melbourne, Australia, for rest and recovery and arrived on December 29.

Many of the men are in really bad shape because of numerous jungle diseases and infections. Medical personnel said that over five thousand treatment cases came into the Melbourne hospital during the first few weeks after we arrived. However, Billy and I did pretty well in that area, and I think it was because of all those mosquitoes that bit us in Prairie. Both of us got treated for dysentery and jungle rot anyway, and we were released from the hospital a few days ago. Please tell Annie that Billy is doing great and so am I, now that we've both had a bath. Many others are improving from their illnesses, as well.

We don't know how long we will be here. I know it is going to take some of the men a long time to recover, though, if they ever do. However, a rumor was that we would be here until the last man leaves the hospital. Someone else said it would be until the last man died from his illness. Personally, I don't think it will be either one of those. I think when Uncle Sam has a big need for able-bodied men, he'll call up those of us who can serve, and we will be sent out again to another battle. There are a lot more islands to conquer (they call this island hopping) before we get to Japan.

I miss all of you very much and am praying to God to stop the war so we can get on with our lives in peace and love.

Ezell

November 25, 1944

Dear Papa, Mama, and Rose,

I thought for sure all of us who were soon on the mend from Guadalcanal were going to be fighting again this summer in Rabaual, but for some reason, the Allied military leaders canceled the invasion of that island. Instead, our air force started bombing the heck out of the Japanese base there. About one hundred thousand Japanese waited for a land invasion that never came. Our bombers also pounded their ships, submarines, and aircraft. Remember I told you about the strategy called "island hopping"? We, along with our Allies, did this all along the islands in the Central Pacific, passing by the Japanese strongholds and invading the islands that were more weakly held. That strategy became known as "leapfrogging," and it took us across the Gilbert, Marshall, Caroline, and Marianna Islands. Because we did it so much, we became experts at amphibian invasions. Seaborne operations also included land, air, and naval fighting. Because of leapfrogging, each island that was captured became the base from which the next island was struck. Pretty good strategy, huh?

We invaded the Gilbert Islands in November 1943 and were able to capture this tiny island in four days. The Allies improved their amphibian operations because of lessons learned on the Gilbert Islands. So, fewer of our men died in the coming invasions.

The Marshall Islands were next. It came easier, with only six hundred of our men killed and eleven thousand of the Japanese. The Allied leadership decided to skip the Japanese naval base on Turk Island and go into the Caroline Islands, where we were again victorious.

In early November, air force B-29 bombers were striking hard at the home base of Japan from their base in the Mariana Islands. Before the invasion of the Philippines, a final hop in September this year took us soldiers to Palau Island. These islands were between the Marianas and the Philippines, with most of the fighting taking place on the small island of Peleliu.

CHAPTER NINE

The War Continued

September 26, 1944

Dear Mom, Dad, and Rose,

*W*e've all been suffering almost unbearable heat here on Peleliu Island since it is closest to the equator. Even at night it never gets below 100 degrees. And it gets up to 120 degrees in the daytime. If any of us ever gets a sore or is wounded, it will get infected and never heal. Japanese corpses lying on the coral quickly decompose in the heat and cause a terrible stench. It lasts for weeks on end, and we can never escape it. Since the island is made of coral, there isn't enough soil to even dig graves.

While we were there, I heard that one of the men from the small town in Texas was planning to write a book about the Peleliu battle. His name is R. V. Burgin. I hope he can do it, because it is hard enough to write letters home about the battles when it isn't this hot. I'm doing it, though, because I want all of you to know what it is really like over here. I would like to know why Burgin is writing; it's probably because he has someone back home that he loves too.

When I finally got a chance to talk with Burgin, he told me that if he didn't write a book about Peleliu and the brave American men that fought and died here, no one would ever know anything about this part of the Pacific War. Burgin said everyone would know about all the other islands, because news journalists went to the other islands that weren't as hot as this one and sent information home daily.

Did I tell you when I was writing from Guadalcanal that I also met some Navajo Indians from Arizona? They were known as code talkers, and they arrived in Guadalcanal not long after we did in 1942. In fact, they seem to be everywhere in the Pacific. They faced as much, if not more, discrimination as we colored soldiers did. Not so much because of their color, but because they looked so much like the Japanese. Sometimes, it was difficult to tell them apart. Some of them actually were assigned bodyguards. The Indians were patriotic and brave in winning our Pacific battles. We didn't hear much about their role in World War I. They were Choctaws then and kept their contribution a secret for twenty years after the war. However, German "scholars" and "tourists" in the 1920s and 1930s came to this country and studied the language extensively—all but the Navajo.

Looks like these Indians will keep their secret for the next twenty years too. They didn't talk much about what they did, and they were quiet when they were hurt or wounded. They remained silent, as Indian warriors were taught to do from birth. Jimmy King, their leader, said there would not be any parades or ceremonies when they arrived home. "No one will know anything about what we did, and we will never talk about it. We will go back to our families and communities just like nothing ever happened," King said.

There's some good folks around the United States, just like there are around Monroe and Lowndes County. Besides little things like bragging and how we show our emotions, we are all pretty much alike. It's just like you always told me, Papa: Every single one of us bleed red. Even the Japanese women mourn and cry for their dead sons and husbands.

Love to all,

Ezell

February 17, 1945

Dear Papa, Mama, and Rose,

We are getting close to Japan. Our men, along with the all Allies, are fighting now in the China Burma Indian Theater. While America planes are dropping bombs on Japanese cities, our units have orders to invade Iwo Jima, a small volcanic island about 750 miles south of Japan. It is called Sulfur Island by the Japanese because of its bad odor. It was defended by more Jap soldiers than I had ever seen before, and they were prepared to fight to the death. The island was bombed a long time before we got there, but the results have been of little effect. The island people had a great many underground tunnels, one so big that it housed a hospital. We said that the Japanese were not just *on* the island, they were *in* it.

Lots of Love,

Ezell

P.S. On February 23, some of the guys put our flag up Mount Sarabachi. Several of our men gave their lives to do this. In reality they were boys, all under the age of twenty. Lives were lost because it meant fighting the Japs all the way up the mountain to plant the flag. The mountain belonged to us, but not the island yet. Fighting continued through March and April on the 8 square-mile island. It turned out to be a bloody battle fought by the marines and some army men …

* * * * *

This was something I knew I couldn't share with the folks back home, but I wanted to write it down so that every detail would be clear in my mind when I got home.

Billy and I were both on the front lines of one of the last battles of Iwo Jima. Billy was about 30 yards in front of me when a bullet hit him and he went down. I saw him fall, and I knew I had to cross heavy fire to reach him and bring him back behind our lines. I ran in a zigzag pattern as fast as I could go, praying all the while that a bullet wouldn't hit me too. When I finally reached him, I lifted him up and put him over my shoulder, then turned and ran for our line as fast as I could. Billy was moaning as I ran, and I took this as a good sign that he was still alive. When I got back behind our lines, I yelled for a medic. Before I barely had gotten the first yell out, the medic arrived. He took Billy from me and said, "Your friend here is in the best hands you could hope for; he's going to get well. Now I suggest you get back in the battle 'cause they need men like you." I said, "Yes, sir," and turned around to run to help to other guys who needed me more than Billy did.

Later, Billy told me what had gone on between him and the medic. Billy said, "Ezee, this white man looked me straight in the eyes and said, 'Son, you aren't going to die! I'm Dobbie James, and I've never lost a man yet. You're just lucky you got me, because I'll have you as good as new in no time. You're my man, and I have faith in you.' " Then Billy added, "Lord knows that Doc James meant every word he said. He cared about me, and I stopped being 'fraid rit then. He stopped the bleeding, cleaned out the hole and all 'round it, then he sterilized it and gave me some kind of injection, so as I wouldn't get an infection, he told me. When I asked him what'd happened, he looked at me again and lightly slapped me on my good shoulder, told me that the very first thing he did was an assessment (whatever that means), then he di'nosed me as having a 'through and through' shoulder wound. He used them big words to me just like he thought I would know them. Now ain't that a sight! If I ever see Doc James again, I want to tell him that he's jus about the first white man I's ever liked. Oh, and another thing, Ezee, that man told me that you was probably gonna get some kind of medal to wear on your uniform for what you done in bringing me back over to our side. Do you know what he was talking about?"

"Can't say that I do, Billy, but I'll probably find out before long."

* * * * *

March 25, 1945

Dear Mama, Papa, and Rose,

Our next battle will be on island "X." Pretty much everyone knows where it will be by now. Yes, it's Okinawa. Seems that each one of their places get harder to conquer than the last. Guess it's because the Japanese already know where we are headed. Tokyo Rose and all those other sultry voiced women who broadcast in her name are telling the Allies and the Japs that they are winning the war. Of course we know better, but most of the Japs, especially the civilians, don't. I think this is the last battle in which Billy and I will be fighting. Please tell Annie—or read to her some of the things I write—so she will know about Billy. Billy has grown up so much, as have I, since we left home. We are both looking out for each other now so much of the time. When I get home, I'll tell you of an event that is a perfect example of this. I can't send it in a letter because it would just be censored. Guess a lot of my mail is censored anyway.

Okinawa is 18 miles across and 60 miles long and is less than 360 miles from Japan. The Japanese spent many years preparing for its defense, so you can imagine how well they are entrenched underground. On April 1, 1945, we went ashore, and the combat began immediately. We were against overwhelming odds of Japanese who were fighting desperately from fortified caves, camouflaged pits, trenches, and concrete bunkers. The fighting was savage, and after eighty-two days, Okinawa surrendered. It was one of the bloodiest battles in Marine Corps history in terms of lives lost in the Pacific. Five sailors and twenty-two marines were awarded the Medal of Honor for their bravery. After this, the planning was underway for the invasion of Japan.

A good example of this savage fighting was the other night when Billy and I were both in the same foxhole. It was pitch dark, and everything was quiet. Each night we all took turns doing the watch. It was spooky because the night was black and the jungle, thick. All kinds of noises were out there, and we could never tell if it was an iguana or a Jap soldier. We fed mosquitoes all night long, every night. We have been living on the storage of rice and oats that the Japs had left behind for a long time. Before long, we were all sick and exhausted, as well as being on edge. Switching off every two hours with the guy in the same foxhole did not give either of us much sleep, and this night we were both wide awake and pretty nervous. Something was going to happen. A big gun went off in our area, and then there was a flash! We both saw a Jap soldier in the foxhole in front of us, chopping off the heads of two of our men. The darkness came again, and then another flash again! We saw the Japanese soldier already in our foxhole standing right between us, with his sword raised high over his head, almost ready to come down on one of us. Darkness! Billy nudged. We shot. The sound of a scream and a thud—one or both of us hit him, and he fell before doing to us what he had just done to the other two men. We shook while sitting there in complete silence for what seemed to be an eternity ... before the next flash. There he laid ... at our feet. Him or us. Our closest call! "Praise the Lord," we both said at the same time.

Love,

Ezell and Billy

P.S. Before signing off, I have something else I want to tell you. When the bullets were flying the worst yesterday, I saw a man, a medic, working right out in the middle of the whole thing—completely unarmed. The other medics usually carry a handgun, but not this one. Of course, I asked around about him and learned he was a conscientious objector and had refused to carry any kind of weapon. Seems he had told his commanding officer that he had joined to "save lives—not to take them." This resulted in his suffering all kinds of ridicule and abuse from the other men in his platoon. The guys had called him names such as coward, wimp, and even yellow. They played tricks on him and made up stories about him. One of the officers even tried his best to get him discharged. This young man was from Lynchburg, Virginia, and his name was Desmond Doss.

When fighting started in Okinawa, I was told that the attitude of the soldiers toward Doss began to change. Desmond Doss was no longer an outcast—in fact, he became a hero, saving the lives of hundreds of fighting men. He never stopped plunging ahead into enemy territory to drag wounded men back to the medical unit. Once, when there were seventy-five wounded men trapped behind enemy lines on a steep cliff, Desmond had a rope and lowered each man down the cliff, one at a time, to a waiting ambulance below. Another time when Desmond was wounded, he bandaged his bleeding arm and then crawled, arm over arm, for several hours until they reached the medical unit outpost. He had refused to be carried on the stretcher because he said there were others who needed it.

Fighting was so intense in Okinawa that Doss lost the small Bible that his wife had given him. Unknown to Doss, after the battle was over, every man in the battalion searched the ground until they found the Bible. When it was returned to him, it was torn and charred. It meant so much to him that tears came to his eyes.

Later, we all heard President Truman awarded him the Medal of Honor for bravery.

Will write again soon.

Love and kisses,

Ezell

It was after Ezell returned home that he told us, "Sergeant Randolph called our company together to discuss the matter of going home. He told all of us that a ship was coming close enough to Okinawa to stop for some of the men who had earned enough points to go home. Because of having served in active duty in Peleliu, Guadalcanal, Iwo Jima, and in Okinawa, Billy and I were both eligible to return home on this ship. Most of the other men would go on to help in China. Billy and I and a few others were to be replaced by newer troops coming in from Canada. It was no longer a rumor but a reality that felt too good to be true, but Sergeant Randolph assured us it was true. We were going home for real, and we were—after all those islands, fighting, and killing—still alive.

* * * * *

"Goin' home. Just wait till I tell Rose, Mama, and Papa," I said, talking to myself.

Just about that time, Billy ran up, almost knocking me over, threw his arms around me, and then broke down in sobs combined with spurts of laughter. "Sorry, Ezee, but I's so happy, jus can't keep it to myself."

"Hey, what? What can't you keep?"

"I's 'shamed, but I can't help crying."

"Nothing wrong with crying, Billy."

"But we is fighting men, Ezee, not crybabies."

"To heck with that, Billy. Anybody that fought like you did… Why, you're the bravest man I ever saw—except for Desmond Doss—and that just makes you the second-most. Now you shut up, and let's start getting ready to go home."

"Thanks, Ezee, guess I'm a pretty good fighter man. I was so scared, I figured the more of dem Japs—specially the ones up in them trees— that I got rid of, the fewer there'd be to shoot at me, and you, of course."

"Thanks, Billy! You shot so many, that they were falling all around me most of the time we were out there in the jungle. How did you do that?"

"Well, it's like this: Uncle Jimmy taught me how to shoot squirrels up in the trees. He said to me, 'Never mind them squirrels on the ground; they're either sickly or old. Get them up in the trees, whether they's a-sittin', or running, or flying, and they'll be tasty, young, and tender meat for eaten.' Ain't never forgot that, neither. He went on to say, 'For every one you get to go in the toe sack, I'll give you one of them shiny nickels too.' So I never forgot what he said about them squirrels being good eaten, and boy howdy, they was! 'Sides that, I made enough money one fall to buy me a little radio. That's how I learned those tunes I play on my harmonica, Ezee."

"I understand why you shoot the squirrels, but how did you get so good at doing it? How did you hit those Japs like you did? They were camouflaged, and you still spotted them, and you hit them every time you shot," I said.

"Ezee, them squirrels were camouflaged too. They was brown, jus like the tree trunks was. We didn't have much money to spend on bullets, so I learned to hit them every time I shot. I didn't do dat at first, tho," Billy replied.

He continued, "Uncle Jimmy picked out the tallest tree and climbed up it with a little can of red paint and a painting brush tied around his waist. When he got part way up, he sat down on a limb and painted a red circle on the tree trunk. Then he climbed down that tall ole tree and said, 'Shoot it, boy.' So I shot at it and missed the whole red circle. Ain't that a sight! Then he walked over to me and showed me how. 'Position the rifle on your shoulder by putting the stock against you shootin' shoulder.' Then he told me to look down through the rear sights to the front sight, lining up the target right on top of the front site. Now comes the most important part. Uncle Jimmy said, 'Ain't none of that gunna do you no good ifens you don't ever so gently and ever so softly squeeze that trigger right, with no fast movement here, no jerking, or nutin—just gently squeeze it. You got that?' I fired the gun, and I got inside the circle that time. Uncle Jimmy said, 'It ain't good nuff,' and I shot again and again till he'd finally say, 'Bull's-eye.' Me and Uncle Jimmy spent days doin' this, Ezee, and I don't know if it was fun or work—both, I think.

"Anyway, it went on till I could shoot a very small circle up real high. Then he started hidin' them circles under leaves jus like the squirrels would hide when they know folks was around shootin' at 'em. I got real good at this, and right before squirrel season. Ain't that a sight! One day, Uncle Jimmy brought a big ole toe sack for me to put the squirrels in. I filled it 'bout half full the very first day. Well, the next few days I was shootin' more squirrels, and the sacks got more stuffed. We started sellin' them squirrels for 30 cents a squirrel, 'cause they was more tender and better than any of the other fellows could shoot. Ain't that a sight!" Billy said.

"Your uncle was a real smart man to pick you out of his whole family of boys, and he knew how to teach well, too," I said.

"Sho was. You know something, Ezee? It was a whole lot easier shootin' them Japs off of the trees than it was them poor little squirrels," replied Billy.

All we had to do now was to wait for the ship to come by Okinawa to drop off our replacements, pick us up, and head for home.

CHAPTER TEN

Return to the USA

*W*ithin a few weeks, Ezell and Billy were on board the *USS Inger-soll*, headed for the United States. Those days aboard the ship were nowhere near as regimented as it had been going over there. They were able to spend time talking with each other, writing, creating music, and practicing it together. Every time they played and sang, the troops gathered around to listen. Many people on the ship knew Billy and Ezell. They had time to talk with the other men this time. They talked about the flag raising on Iwo Jima, as well as the interesting people they had met: the Navajo code talkers; R. V. Burgin, the author of *Island of the Damned*; Desmond Doss, the heroic conscientious objector; and others.

While aboard the ship on the morning of July 17, there was a ship-wide broadcast of what had happened the day before back home. It seemed that President Roosevelt had learned from a special advisory committee, based on research that had been going on since 1939, that uranium was much more destructive than any known explosives. He decided to find out more about uranium, and hired physicist Dr. J. Robert Oppenheimer to lead a top-secret scientific experiment to study the matter.

On that day in 1945, Dr. Oppenheimer and other scientists were ready to do some testing of the weapon, and the first test of the atom bomb took place in the deserts of New Mexico. When the explosion took place, the blast blew out windows of homes nearly 100 miles away. There was a mushroom-looking cloud that went up 40,000 feet over the desert. Several people who saw it said it was both magnificent and humbling. Dr. Oppenheimer stated that a line from the Bhagavad Gita came into his mind: "I have now become death—the destroyer of worlds." The test was successful beyond the expectation of anyone.

July 28, 1945

If there wasn't news enough while still on board the *USS Ingersoll*, another ship-wide radio announcement was broadcast. Churchill, Stalin, and Truman (President Roosevelt had died) met at Potsdam, Germany, on July 17 to discuss postwar boundaries, as well as the future of Japan.

Because of the experiences they had fighting the Japanese, they knew how fatalistic and tenacious the Japanese were. The Allies were also aware that any operations would cost large numbers of American and British lives—perhaps as many as millions.

President Truman, the day before the meeting, had learned of the success of the atomic bomb test in New Mexico. This gave President Truman just what he needed to bargain with the senate. So on July 26, Churchill, Truman, and Chiang Kai-shek of the Nationalist Government of China signed the Potsdam Declaration. This declaration called for the unconditional surrender of Japan. It stated in detail the terms of surrender and all of the stipulations that would follow, including the occupation of the Allied forces and that Japan would have a democratic form of government with control limited to their home islands only; none of their colonies were to be included. Japan refused to accept the Allied terms of surrender, drawn up and signed by all the other warring nations.

The *USS Ingersoll* had made top speeds across the Pacific and was getting closer to the US each day that passed. The arrival date was set for July 30 in New Orleans, and it looked like they would be right on time. Ezell and Billy had already arranged to take the train out of New Orleans straight into Aberdeen, where Uncle John, Aunt Nettie, Annie, Rose, and I would be waiting for them. Or, I *thought* Rose would be there waiting too.

* * * * *

But when they arrived in Aberdeen, after our joyous greetings, we all realized only one thing was missing and that was—Rose.

Ezell asked Aunt Nettie why Rose wasn't with them, and she replied that they hadn't seen Rose for several weeks. Aunt Nettie added that when she had called Rose to invite her to go along with them, Rose had thanked her and said, with no explanation as to why not, that she wouldn't be going. Aunt Nettie exclaimed she thought that was strange but didn't want to pry into Rose's business.

"Don't you have any idea as to what is wrong with Rose?" Aunt Nettie asked.

"No, Mama," Ezell said, "But I do know that I haven't been getting any letters from her, and that's just not like my Rose. I always got about three or four letters from her every week until about a month ago, when they started dropping off gradually to none. I'm worried, Mama. I feel like I've lost my sweetheart."

"Honey, I don't have any answers for you, but I simply can't imagine anything like that could happen—not between you two. It just doesn't make sense," Aunt Nettie replied.

"Well, I'm going to find out why, just as soon as I get home," Ezell said with determination. After a moment of silence, Ezell spoke again: "Billy and I have arranged to go from here to Prairie on the bus, and we'll be seeing you at home. When you have the celebration dinner, can Billy come too?"

"Of course he can. A friend of yours is a friend of ours. We'll do the preparations. We'll have some of your favorite foods, honey. There'll be those wonderful, tasty, good-smelling yeast rolls with butter, grilled pork loin, garden-fresh green beans, the mashed potatoes you like so much, and the old-fashioned rhubarb pie that came from your papa's mother. I printed out each of the recipes for our guests to try, if they would like. Mr. and Mrs. Bean, our new friends, will be here, too, as will Annie's new friend Micah. You haven't met Micah yet, because we hired him after you left. I'm glad he and Annie have become friends, for heaven knows, he must need someone with whom to talk to because most of the workmen are afraid of him, and sweet little Annie is lonely too."

"Why are they afraid of him, Mama?"

"I don't know for sure, but Annie told me that one of the workers had started a rumor about him, but I think it's just because he's so big that he's almost frightening. Too, Micah usually has a serious look on his face, so he looks scary. Oh, Ezell dear, let's just give him the benefit of the doubt. He has been so helpful to your papa, who really likes him. In fact, John said that he was one of our very best workers as far as knowing his trade, and probably our most loyal one too. I'm just glad he's here. He has done a wonderful job with the landscaping and has even started on the grounds around the new plantation home, as well. Inside our new home, he has repainted the walls all over the house and repaired a number of things. I couldn't be more pleased with what he has done in beautifying that place; it hadn't been done for a long time, and it was beginning to look run down. Why, we'll be moving over there before the end of the month."

"Mama, which evening will you have the dinner?"

"This Friday evening should give everyone enough time to make plans to attend."

"I'll take care of telling Rose, since I'll be going over to her house straight away. Is that alright with you?" Ezell asked.

Aunt Nettie replied, "Of course, but I'll send her an invitation anyway. I know you will get everything straightened out between the two of you."

* * * * *

True to his word, Ezell headed straight for Rose's house. Ezell knocked on the door, and Rose answered. "Hello, Ezell," she calmly said, "I heard you were home. Did you bring her with you?"

"Bring who with me? What are you talking about, Rose?"

"I'm talking about the woman you met when you were overseas, of course."

"I didn't meet any woman, Rose. Why did you think that?"

"Because you quit writing to me."

"No! I didn't quit writing to you. I wrote once or twice a week until I got home. What caused you to think that, and why did you stop?"

"I didn't quit writing to you, either."

"Then what happened? Now I need to find out what happened to my letters to you. No telling how many, either."

"Ezell, do you think they may have been lost or just not sent out by the military?"

"No way! That wouldn't have happened. Maybe one or two at the most—if one of the ships carrying mail was sunk. No, somebody around here must have been intercepting those letters I wrote. So why?"

"My mother has always been afraid I would leave her ... get married, you know ..." Rose stammered at the realization of what had happened to her. "Oh my goodness, Ezell! I bet it was my mother that did this. She's getting old and more afraid of being left alone every day. Poor Mama, but I guess I haven't been able to convince her. Oh Ezell, I'm so sorry."

"It's alright, Rose. I'm just glad you believed me and started thinking what could have happened. Now, can we get on with our plans and life together?"

"Not right away, I'm afraid. See, I started dating a new fellow from Louisiana that moved in here with the Gulf Ordinance Plant. He lives over in one of the block houses that the government built for their administrative people. His name is Roel. He's part African-American and part French. I'm not in love with him like I am with you, Ezell. I—"

"That's all I need to know, Rose, my love. Don't say anymore. I know what you are telling me. I'll be back for you later to go to the celebration dinner with me, and we'll announce our engagement then."

"Where are you going?"

"To talk to Roel, that's where."

"Oh my goodness, Ezell ... Can't we just forget about him?"

"Don't think so, love."

"Please be careful, Ezell."

So Ezell walked over to Roel's home, hoping he would have the opportunity of talking to him face-to-face or fist-to-fist ... either way, it didn't matter to him.

Knocking rather loudly on Roel's front door, Ezell stood and waited. In a few minutes, Roel came to the door and said, "Can I help you?"

Quickly, Ezell spoke, "You can help yourself and keep from getting hurt badly by leaving my girl, Rose, alone. I'm Ezell Oldham, and I've been away for a while serving my country, but now I'm home again, and

Rose and I will be continuing our relationship. Before long, we'll be getting married. Do you understand?"

"Surely do, Mr. Ezell. I thought she was too fine a person not to be a married woman. So the two of you plan to be married soon?"

"Yes, sometime before this month is over."

"Then I wish you well," Roel said. "Hope you'll accept my apologies for taking Rose out a few times. It certainly won't happen again now that I've seen ... uh, met you, Mr. Ezell."

"Name's Oldham. Ezell. Jefferson. Oldham."

"Well, like I said, Mr. Jefferson Oldham, it won't happen again."

* * * * *

From up here on the second floor, I can see nearly the whole plantation! There goes Ezell back to Rose's house again. Wish I knew what was going on. Now Rose is all dressed up so pretty, and they seem to be headed for our house. Wonder why? Oh, oh, it's Friday, and this is the day we are having the celebration dinner. I'm supposed to be in the kitchen, too, making that rhubarb pie. I better get dressed and get down those stairs right away. I hope nobody noticed I wasn't down there helping.

Oops, nobody's even started on the pie. I better get moving. The kitchen and dining room are filled with the most wonderful smells, but there's nothing to compare with the smell of those yeast rolls rising. They make my mouth water whenever the oven door is open. After I get that pie in the oven, I need to go into the living room and greet Aunt Nettie and Uncle John's new friends. I like them, but they talk funny—guess it's because they are from up north. I don't care about that, though, 'cause some of us talk funny, too, especially Billy. Though I've noticed he speaks much better now than he did before he left for the war. Uncle John said things like traveling tended to help people speak better and broaden their minds too. He should know, because he traveled a lot when he went overseas in World War I. Maybe someday I can travel, too, as well as get a college education like Aunt Nettie did ... Hope so.

Oh, Aunt Nettie and Uncle John's friends are talking to Billy and Ezell. They are all laughing and talking and having a good time. I'll just try to ease in and say hello while my pie finishes baking. Love that nice music that Aunt Nettie has softly playing in the background. Better go into the living room and say hello to the Beans and introduce myself to Mr. Bean and Billy's girlfriend. I'm so glad Aunt Nettie and Uncle John will have friends again so they will be able to go places and do things with another couple. Aunt Nettie told me that Uncle John and Mr. Bean had already made plans to go to the fall horse show in West Point. That means I'll get to go too!

For this dinner, Aunt Nettie has placed cards at each place setting with each person's name on them. She has a nice menu card at each setting, too, as well as a large flower arrangement in the center of the table. All that silver that was in Uncle John's family is around each of the nicest china plates, and just above the silverware, someone has placed the pretty crystal glasses just perfectly. I love to look at all the little sparkles of light from the crystal reflecting on the white tablecloth. Aunt Nettie says that the presentation, whatever that means, is just as important as the food that is being served. It really does look beautiful; I'm so glad now that she taught me how to do all this. Someday, maybe I'll be able to do it for people and a man who will enjoy it like I do …

All kinds of announcements were made at the dinner tonight. Uncle John told everyone of his plans to move up the road a few miles to another plantation. "It's really a small farm this time, because I may be retiring after this one," Uncle John said. Then Ezell and Rose told of their plans to marry in August, and Billy proudly introduced his new girlfriend. Micah and Annie were happy together, and everyone had a great time.

That year Ezell and Rose were married. They had planned to marry soon after his arrival home from the war. They were married on September 25, 1945. It was a beautiful autumn day with near-perfect weather. After the marriage, they moved to the little college town of Cleveland, Mississippi, where Rose had a good teaching job and Ezell found work as a mechanic right after they arrived. Life was very good for the married couple.

Earlier that summer we moved from the large plantation in Prairie to the smaller one out from Aberdeen. A young lady by now, I had once more made that trip from Sulligent, Alabama, to Aberdeen, Mississippi. As always, Uncle John and Aunt Nettie were waiting for me at the same train station in Aberdeen. We all hugged each other, then got into Uncle John's little blue Ford to head for home. I had anticipated another good summer, but this was not to be.

When I arrived at the new plantation, I saw that it was much smaller and less beautiful than Lenoir. This was quite a surprise to me. It no longer seemed like a plantation mansion, but just a nice home. I decided that was alright, however, since my Uncle John and Aunt Nettie were there and that's what made it a home, anyway. Annie, the cook my aunt and uncle had had at Lenoir, came along with them, and I loved Annie almost as much as Aunt Nettie. The new person on the scene was Micah—big, tall Micah, who did the landscaping and took care of the house on the outside, as well as doing a few indoor repairs and painting.

Uncle John made his rounds of the new plantation on his big black stallion, just as he had before we moved. Although life seemed to return to normal, I had an uneasy feeling. Something just didn't seem right. Something unsettling was in the air, and I knew Uncle John felt it too. Maybe that's why he told me a story about Luther Weems more than once. Luther Weems was the previous plantation manager at the new place, and he had been quite displeased that he had been fired and that Uncle John had been hired in his place. It seemed that Luther had always been in trouble because of his drunken rages and his tendency to get into fights. In short, he was just a mean man who had let the plantation go down. The owner had delayed in firing him for some time, but the day he met Uncle John, the owner decided he had waited long enough. He offered my uncle the job but didn't tell Luther. I think it was because he was just plain afraid to.

Luther heard of it in a day or two and was just furious about it. He kept telling the workmen that John Oldham would be sorry he had ever "taken the job away" from Luther. Uncle John just ignored that and kept on doing what the owner, Mr. Norton, had told him he wanted done during Uncle John's first month there. It seemed to bother me more than it did Uncle John. It was probably because my parents had taught me to be afraid of drunk men, and I had seen Mr. Weems around the place drunk and acting a fool. I just wasn't used to seeing anything like that, so I was really afraid for Uncle John. Maybe Uncle John saw this and sought to get my mind off of it by telling me that "blowhards" seldom did anything but make noise—and how would I like to drive his car?

"Oh, Uncle John, that would be wonderful," I said. "You'll be right beside me, though, won't you?"

"Of course, Baby Girl," Uncle John said, "Guess I better stop calling you that, though, because you are getting all grown up now. You didn't think I'd be riding Big Ben and leaving you to learn by yourself, did you?"

"No, Uncle John, I just thought I needed to get everything nailed down, though, because I'm a little shaky about trying it."

"You'll do fine, Baby ... Avla," he said, correcting himself.

"When do we start?" I asked.

"How about now?" Uncle John laughingly said. "But I need to tell Micah and Jim down there that we will be away from the farm for about thirty minutes to an hour. You run up to the house and tell your Aunt Nettie. She already knows I was going to help you today, so that'll be no problem there," said Uncle John.

"Okay, Uncle John! Will do!" I ran up the little hill to the house, told her, and ran back down to where the car was parked as fast as I could—for fear that Uncle John might change his mind or get too busy to do it.

He was there at the car door waiting for me with that usual broad smile on his face, which had a way of reassuring and calming me down.

"Let's go, Uncle John!" I yelled.

"You can't drive on that side of the car," he said. "Get around over here and under the wheel."

As I slid in on the driver's side and under the wheel, I thought, *Oh my gosh, this is it.*

"Wait just a minute for me. I have to tell Micah one more thing," Uncle John said.

CHAPTER ELEVEN

He Shot My Uncle!

J looked back in the rear-view mirror and could see Uncle John walking back behind the car to talk with Micah again. Then another man
stepped out in front of Micah. He looked like Luther Weems. It was
Luther Weems, and the two were talking—Uncle John quietly, and
Luther yelling, cursing, and flailing his arms.

I thought, *Looks like he's carrying a gun. Why in the world would he be
carrying that?*

Uncle John turned around to walk back to the car, and about that
time I heard a *-boom!-*. The shot hit Uncle John. He fell face-forward on
the ground, and a pool of blood began to form on the ground.

Luther has shot my Uncle John, I thought, *and for no reason, either. He
shot him in the back. This can't be happening! I'll take this car and run right
over Luther. I'll teach him to shoot my Uncle John …*

"You're dead meat, Luther Weems!" I shouted at the top of my
lungs while stepping just a few inches outside the car, so he could hear
me. "I'll run this car right over you and flatten you like roadkill if it's the
last thing I ever do. Do you hear me, Luther? You'll be sorry you ever
heard of John Oldham, you coward! You murderer! Just you wait and
see!"

At that point, I jumped in the car and attempted to start it but must
have flooded it. While I was waiting for it to start, I thought about getting
my uncle in the car and taking him to the hospital. I yelled for Micah and
Jim to help me get Uncle John in the car; they were already running
toward him to try to pick him up the easiest way possible, all the while
telling me that he wasn't dead, he was just filled with buckshot and had
lost consciousness.

We got him in, and this time, the car started. Luther was now running for the woods up ahead of the car, through the cotton patch, behind
the barn. I still wanted to kill him, so I went after him, thinking maybe I

could kill him real fast and still get Uncle John to the hospital emergency room, three and a half miles away, before he died—or something. The little car didn't do very well going over those rows of cotton. It really slowed me down with all the bouncing and jolting, once almost turning over. The bouncing was terrible, and the dust was beginning to cloud my vision. By this time, I couldn't see a thing for the cloud of dust rising both in front and behind the car. The car was still running, however, and I gunned it and miraculously got it turned around and out onto the highway, headed toward Aberdeen. Little did I know that someone else was chasing Luther Weems too.

The sharp cracking of branches under the runner's feet, the noise of somebody behind him running hard and fast, breathing heavily. His own breath was coming in short bursts, and his lungs filled with damp air and the molding smells from the woods. His anguished mind was filled with thoughts of the violence that had recently happened and of how he could escape. The sudden roar of a car engine being gunned caught slightly in his awareness.

The runner entered the woods and became lost in the darkness, feeling a wave of terror washing over him by the grave-like coldness that seemed to be pulling him onward and downward. Though exhausted from having run so far, he kept on running with limited vision because of the sharp contrast between the bright sunlight of the fields and the cool darkness of the woods. A few more yards, and he tripped over something. Throwing his hands out blindly before him, he fell forward into a puddle of something that felt like soft mud. The smell of decaying flesh assaulted his nostrils immediately, then his senses, too, causing his eyes to water and his hands to feel disgustingly warm and sticky. With dawning horror, he realized that what his hands were in was not a mound of mud at all, but the decaying body of a small animal. In the dim light, he made out a set of wide-open eyes and then recoiled as he saw a ginger-colored tail, white-tipped and mangled. The overwhelming dread of never being able to get his hands clean again was almost more than his fragmented and fearful mind could bear. Finding a stream or a source of running water was all he could think about for several minutes of time—time he did not have if he had any plans of saving his own life from that huge, dark figure of a person that had been pursuing him for such a long time, for so many years ... years when he had felt blood splashing on his hands from his own brutality—all of those that he had pursued with the dogs at his side until he had finally run them down. Now he no longer knew if he was the pursuer or the runner. Being either no longer mattered to him. His mind no longer told him that he was being pursued and that he needed to run because his life depended on it. He finally started seeing shadows dart from one tree to another, shadows of strange monkey-like-looking people. He found a little stream in which to wash his hands, to try to wash all the blood off and all the stench of dead bodies that he, along with other men like him, had buried in those very dark woods.

"God help me!" was his last cry as he felt hands go around his body and lift him high above the ground where the air was now heavy, where it was so difficult to breathe, so difficult to scream for help, which he in some way knew was a futile effort. Fists pounding, with the pain beginning to leave ... Sounds and smells drifting away ... Day turning into night, and nothing left but darkness. Nothing left ... of the runner/pursuer/decomposing and dying bodies. All darkness. All *nothingness* ...

* * * * *

I kept my car window open so I could wave and yell at the people driving on the highway to get out of my way. Too, I used the horn a lot and drove as fast as I could. I wished I had started sooner because by now, Uncle John was regaining consciousness. He was doing a lot of moaning and groaning. I was able to keep the car pretty much on the road, only running off two or three times. Nothing mattered to me now but getting my uncle to the hospital.

Micah musta thought I knew how to drive because he didn't object to me being the one to take Uncle John to the hospital. When Uncle John and I got there, the medics were standing outside the emergency room waiting for us, so they took Uncle John out and put him on their stretcher and took him inside while I parked the car. It was only then that

I noticed how badly my hands were shaking. *I hope there's no policemen or lawmen around*, I thought just before going inside.

The medics had taken Uncle John straight back to the doctors, who gave him a shot for the pain and began the tedious process of trying to pick the pellets out of the holes in Uncle John's skin. I was taken to the hallway to wait until the doctor had finished.

While I was waiting, the Monroe County sheriff walked in and said, "I'm Sheriff Brentman. The hospital called me. I would like to ask you some questions. Is that okay with you?"

My, but he was handsome! "Sure," I said, "I'll tell you what I know."

"Do you know the name of the suspect, and please tell me your name."

"I surely do," I replied. "It was Luther Weems, the previous plantation manager. I'm Alva Jo Hollis from Gattman, just down the road."

"Miss Hollis, this is Officer Carl Smith who just walked in, and he will be helping me with the case," Sheriff Brentman said. "Officer Smith, this is Miss Alva Jo Hollis, and she is an eyewitness. You are late, Officer Smith. I don't want your reason at this time. Now, let's get started again," said Sheriff Brentman. "Miss Hollis knows the name of the suspect. Would you repeat the name, Miss Hollis?"

"Yes, his name is Luther Weems, and please don't call me 'Miss Hollis.' "

"Sorry," Sheriff Brentman replied, "please tell me, if you know it, what kind of gun the suspect carried."

"Yes, it was a single-barrel shotgun."

"Did you see him shoot this gun at Mr. Oldham?"

"Yes, I did. I also saw my uncle fall from the shots."

"How many times do you think the suspect fired at your uncle?"

"One time. He was too scared to reload, I think."

"What did the suspect do after that?"

"He ran for the woods as soon as he heard me yelling at him. Then we got my uncle into the car."

"We? So then, there were other people there?"

"Yes, sir, two men who worked on the farm were there. Micah and Jim. I don't know their last names."

"We'll need to pick up these two men to talk with them. We'll do that when we go out to rope off the crime scene. I'll need you to give me the exact address and distance from town. Okay?"

"Yes, sir."

"What time of day was it?" Sheriff Brentman asked.

"Oh, somewhere close to two in the afternoon," I replied.

"Thank you, young lady. Will you sign your statement? We need to go see if we can get a statement from your uncle now, and from the doctor, too—along with the pieces of buckshot. Then we'll go out to the house within an hour to rope off where this happened. You'll be there by then, won't you?"

"Yes, sir."

"There is a nurse here to check you out and to take you home, since she is getting off now and lives out your way. One of our officers will drive your uncle's car home for you. I heard you had quite a time getting here."

"Oh, yes, sir, but I didn't much want you to know all about that."

"Well, young lady, I'm a lawman at heart. It's my job to know all about my cases, and I generally do. You're not in trouble. In fact, I think you are a very brave young woman. Just keep on being who you are when you grow up."

"Yes, sir, I will. You're a really nice man. You're just swell!"

"Thank you, ma'am. I plan to keep checking on you over the next few years, just to see how you turn out as you get older. You can tell me where you go to high school, if you like, and give me your parents' names, so I can continue being your friend."

"Yes, sir, I'm glad you asked me that, because I only visit here in the summers. I'm going to be taking driver's education this year at the high school in Sulligent, Alabama. My mother, Mrs. Woodie Hollis, is a teacher in Gattman, where we live, and she wanted me to attend Sulligent High School."

"Thank you, ma'am. Officer Smith and I will see you today over at the crime scene at your uncle's home. We'll send a deputy out to stay at your aunt's house, as protection for both you and your aunt, until the man who did this is under arrest. Now, Officer Smith, let's go get those other statements and the pieces of buckshot we need for evidence."

* * * * *

Nurse Pope drove me right up to the door of Aunt Nettie's and Uncle John's new house before she let me out. The deputy was already there, waiting for my arrival. Aunt Nettie was back in the bedroom getting ready to go to the hospital to stay with Uncle John.

Aunt Nettie kissed me goodbye and ran out to get in a very dirty-looking car to go to the hospital. Uncle John had to stay there until his fever went down, which took three days. Annie was there at the house to stay with me. My efforts to get her to go back home were of no avail because my aunt had told her to stay there with me until she returned.

CHAPTER TWELVE

Crime Scene One

rue to his word, Sheriff Brentman was at our house within the hour. Since Micah and Jim were working not very far from the area where the shooting had taken place, he was able to rope off the crime scene exactly. I wanted to go down there, but Annie wouldn't let me go—though she had to hide all my clothes, except my underwear, to stop me. I wanted to see Sheriff Brentman badly—to see how he worked.

A day or so later, the deputy let it slip to Annie that everybody had been looking for Luther Weems and he was nowhere to be found. His house had no signs of anyone having been in it; his rickety old truck was still sitting at his house. Since Uncle John had been shot, Luther hadn't been seen at the bus station or anywhere around town, either. Most thought he was hiding in the woods where we had seen him running that terrible day. I didn't think so, because too many of the workmen on the farm hated him because of the way he had treated them when he was drunk. Annie told me that he had insulted Micah in front of all of the other men one day, and then she said, "I tremble to think of what Micah could do to that little man if he was of a mind to. He thought the world of Mr. Oldham, even though he hadn't known him very long."

I had never seen Annie scared before. She even walked around with a look of dread and fear on her face, and that got me really worried. Was she afraid Luther might show up at our house during the night, I wondered?

Let me tell you about what happened, because it was so scary for both Annie and me. You see, every worker and family member who had been hurt or mistreated by Luther Weems was called to a meeting after supper on the second night he was missing. There were colored people from all around Monroe, Lowndes, and Clay County who came to the gathering. I think all of the colored people from our plantation were down there. They had been informed that there was a call for the African

Death March. A few of the older people knew what that was, as well as the music and words that went with it. A very nice colored man from West Point by the name of Paul Jefferson came. He was the one who organized the march, sent the word out, and even walked with and led the people who wanted to know the old music and the words for singing. The whole purpose of the march, according to Mr. Jefferson, was to scare Luther Weems out of the woods, so he could be dealt with by the law. It wasn't meant to scare anyone but Luther, for they strongly believed he was in the woods.

They all appeared down at the creek. Since it was a dark night with no moon shining, all you could see were fire torches, and the glimmer of pots and pans going down the hill to the creek. Before long, all those torches seemed to burn stronger, with the strangest sound: the African Death March! They began marching up the hill toward the woods. At the entrance to the woods, each torch began to move a good distance away from the others until a long line was formed. Pots and pans began to bang together furiously loud. Every other torch was put out or maybe just disappeared into the woods—I don't know which. Then that wave of torches disappeared, and the sound of the banging was muffled just a little. There were a lot of those torches disappearing into the woods. They were spaced closely enough together, however, I was told, that each could hear his neighbor on either side speak or yell.

Annie and I were in a room huddled together and so frightened at what we had seen and heard that neither could say a word. We were totally silent through the whole thing. Annie's eyes were large, and they did her talking. I'm pretty sure mine looked the same way. I've never been that scared before.

The next day, the hunt was still on. The sheriff came back with more deputies. Still, there was no Luther. The workers on the plantation were scared, and very little work was done, even though there was a deputy still on the farm as a safety precaution. People were very nervous for miles around, afraid because Luther hadn't been caught. This was the talk of the day, and the sheriff's office received numerous calls asking when Luther was going to be caught.

Questions were being asked around the farm about Micah. The last time he had been seen was the day when the shooting had taken place. Those who knew Micah realized he could become a little hot-headed sometimes. Micah didn't like Luther, but then, neither did most of the other workers. Luther had mistreated them and abused some of them, physically and mentally. Luther had some long leather strips that he put knots in and would have a worker remove his shirt, and then Luther would hit him with those strips until he saw blood pouring down. At other times, Luther would curse his workers and yell terrible, insulting words at them …

Then one day, Micah was seen sitting on his porch. Later on that day, he had little to say as the workers were talking about the shooting of Uncle John and about Luther getting away and not being caught. Finally, Micah, or Big Man as he was called, said, "He be caught by somebody."

One of the workers looked at Micah and said, "Man, I hope so. That Luther is a mean bastard!"

The third day, the sheriff got a call from an old man about what his two grandsons had told him. After hearing a few words, the sheriff knew the story had to be checked out. The old man told the sheriff not to come to his house, as there were too many people around. He and his grandsons would meet him at the Missionary Baptist Church, which was located on the road before getting to the plantation. They would be in a cotton wagon.

In no time, the sheriff and his deputies pulled up, and sure enough, there was an elderly gentleman sitting on a buckboard and two youngsters behind him on some hay. As they told the story, the two boys had been going fishing with their dog following them. Instead of taking the long walk to the lake, walking on the field road that ran around the cotton fields, they had taken a short cut and gone through the woods on an old log road. That way, they didn't waste a lot of time. As they had exited the field road onto the old log road, a few hundred feet in the woods, the dog suddenly stopped and started barking at a pile of bushes. He barked and barked, and even the hair on his back stood up. He kept barking and

Field workers in the cotton patch

growling as if something was in the bushes. The boys were scared, as their dog had never done anything like that. The boys walked over to the stack of bushes and saw a pile of fresh dirt under the bushes. Only three days before, they had walked the same road and that stack had not been there. So they ran back to their grandfather's house and told him what they had seen.

Without hesitation, the sheriff had a gut feeling and said, "Let's go, boys. Show me where this place is. You and your granddad can ride with me. We will bring you back to the church after we check out the location. We won't say anything about you or use your names."

As the sheriff's vehicles entered the plantation quarters, traveling down the old road, the old man and his two grandsons slid down a little in the back seat, hoping not to be seen. Soon, they arrived at the location. The sheriff told the boys and the old man to remain near the car as he and his deputies checked the site out. The sheriff knew if this was a crime scene, he didn't need anyone else there in the way.

CHAPTER THIRTEEN

Crime Scene Two

$\mathcal{S}$ heriff Brentman carefully removed the bushes one at a time, until the mound of soil appeared. He noted the soil was fresh. Then the sheriff saw some footprints; he told his deputies to make a sketch and to get the crime scene box out of the patrol car. Using a ruler to mark across the sides, then down the length, Sheriff Brentman noticed that the shoe had a trademark on the heel. Whoever had made that footprint had a very large foot. After they finished, they started removing the soil a little at a time. In one shovel of soil, there was a button about the size of a dime, white in color. This was placed in an evidence bag. The work continued using the same meticulous procedures. The bag was marked with the date, time, location, and officer's initials. They knew with the small mound of soil, they wouldn't have far to go.

Suddenly, there appeared a leg, then a hand, and then the body, face-up. They noticed the shirt was torn, and blood was on it. At that point, they stopped, and the sheriff told the deputies to call the hospital for an ambulance. If one was not available, then to call the funeral home for colored people and ask them to send a hearse with a cot.

One of the deputies dropped off the old man and the two boys back at the church, telling them not to say anything for now. They were to wait for the deputy to come back and show the way for the hearse. The sheriff knew they had a body but couldn't tell if it was Luther, nor how the person had died. He knew the answers would come when an autopsy was done at the hospital. Time seemed to stand still while he waited on the hearse to arrive.

The body was removed and taken to the hospital in Aberdeen. During that time, the sheriff called for the coroner to meet him there to see if it was Luther, and he also asked for two of the plantation workers to come and help identify the body.

The news traveled fast. People began to come to the hospital but were met by deputies. No one was authorized to enter the morgue except those who needed to be there—the sheriff and two plantation workers to identify the body. They mumbled in a low voice that he had it coming, and that this was indeed Luther Weems.

The autopsy revealed Luther's neck had been broken. His face showed that he had been badly beaten. Two teeth were missing. The ruling was that he had been dead for about seventy-two hours, more or less. An act of murder was also ruled.

As the sheriff and his deputies left the hospital, they saw approximately thirty people, mostly just spectators, all talking in low tones. Some were asking the sheriff, "Can you tell us what happened, and is that Luther?" The sheriff only said, "Yes, that's Luther; he is dead." He said nothing more. He knew his work was cut out for him. There was a murder to solve and time was important.

Back to investigating and back to the plantation—the answer had to be there. Someone, somewhere knew and maybe had committed an act of cold-blooded murder, first degree. The big shoe print was the start. Who had a large, large foot? And the answer was fast in coming. After talking to several of the workers, the answer kept coming back to one man they called Big Man. One of the workers told the sheriff that he had seen Micah, Big Man, sitting on his front porch early in the day. The worker said Big Man might still be there but not to tell Big Man that he had told them.

With that information, the sheriff and his chief deputy travelled down the old farm road, seeing Big Man sitting on the front porch in a chair. The sheriff decided to put on an act, so he told his deputy, "Let's just drive by, to see if he runs or goes into the house. Don't wave, just keep your eyes on the road."

Micah saw the dust of the sheriff's vehicle coming toward his house. Seeing there was no indication of the vehicle stopping, he continued sitting there, watching it go by. At the end of the road where there was a turn around, the sheriff said, "Okay, let's go back and stop. I'll wave to Big Man to come out to the car, telling him I was looking for someone but couldn't find them." As the car approached Micah's house, the car stopped and the sheriff waved, saying, "Hey, I need some help and direction. Can you help me?" The sheriff then waved for Micah to come to the car.

As the sheriff got out of the car, Micah waved back and walked toward the dusty road. The deputy sat in the car, watching Micah's every move. *His hands were huge*, the sheriff eyes were saying. "This is Big Man. Look at those shoes, how big, and those arms are very muscular too."

Extending his hand to shake Micah's, the sheriff saw a button was missing on one of his shirt sleeves. Then, as Micah stepped aside to come to the sheriff to shake his hand, the sheriff saw the shoe print in the dust—the heel trademark. Not wanting to show his emotions and trying hard to keep a smile off of his face, the sheriff said, "Micah, you and I need to talk." This was the prearranged signal that the chief deputy was to come out of the car and place handcuffs on the suspect. To the sheriff's amazement, Micah smiled and said, "I'm ready to talk."

As the sheriff's car traveled back down the road in front of the tenant houses, the workers were taking notice of who was in the car as it sped away, leaving behind dust and three days of heartbreak and sadness. Now there was to be a trial and who knew what the verdict would be—maybe even death.

CHAPTER FOURTEEN

Homecoming

*U*ncle John was getting to come home several weeks before Micah's trial. His fever had finally broken, and he was better. Aunt Nettie was so happy to get him back home and take care of him herself. She really loved that man, and she showed it. I loved him, too, but in a different way, just like Ezell taught me about love: It wasn't more or less, just different. That had helped me to understand so much. *When I have children years from now, I hope I still remember that, because—since they will be different from each other— I'm sure I'll love each of them differently too.*

Rose called on the phone and said Ezell had just heard about what had happened to Uncle John and that he was on his way from Cleveland to help out on the plantation. She asked me to tell Aunt Nettie that just as soon as we finished talking over the phone. "Of course I'll tell her, Rose," I said. "She's pretty upset about how Uncle John is not going to be able to work for a while and what will become of them."

The next thing I knew, Rose started crying. "Oh, Alva Jo, I'm so torn up about Ezell and the expression I saw on his face when he heard his papa had been shot in the back. Ezell had often heard about Luther Weems and what he was like, as well. I saw such hatred in his face that I could hardly recognize him. I'm afraid he plans to kill Luther. He has brought so much of the war back with him."

"You know how strong Ezell is, and he'll get that war stuff worked out one way or another. As one of our famous war correspondents, David Wood, wrote of the veterans coming back home even without injuries, 'They all have morale/mental problems to work out. It's the ones who don't have any problems about what they saw and had to do that are scary.' I know you've read or heard about Ernie Pile and David Wood, and that you understand a lot more about what stress can do more than I do, so you just hang in there and keep in touch with us. Because I have gotten to know our local sheriff. Rose, I can assure you that he will get the right man—and soon. So don't you worry so much about Ezell. Sheriff Brentman will get Luther Weems before Ezell even has a chance of doing anything to him; I'll bet my boots on that one."

Rose sniffed. "Ezell got a ride with one of his friends that has the use of a truck this week. Yes, Jo, I am familiar with post-traumatic stress symptoms, and I think that's just what Ezell has now. I've been supporting him the best I know how, mostly listening to him talk to me about some of the rough times over there."

"Take care, Rose. We wish you were coming too."

"So do I, Jo. Love you."

"Bye, now."

* * * * *

"Aunt Nettie! Guess who is coming home besides Uncle John!"

"Yes, Jo, I heard. It will be so nice to have Ezell here to help us until your uncle gets better."

"Yes, it will, and I hope Rose can come too."

"So do I," Aunt Nettie replied.

During my phone conversation with Rose, Aunt Nettie, Micah, and Jim had been moving Uncle John's and Aunt Nettie's bedroom furniture downstairs into the dining room so that Uncle John's room would be the hub of the house. Guess Aunt Nettie would spend some of her time trying to sleep with him and the other part sleeping upstairs in the extra bedroom. I would help all I could too.

After a few hours passed, the doorbell rang, and I quickly recognized the old ring pattern—two shorts and a long—that Ezell always used. "Ezell is here! May I get the door, Aunt Nettie? Please."

"Of course, Jo, but please remember you are a young lady now."

"Alright, Aunt Nettie, I'll remember," I said, but under my breath I was saying, "This 'growing up' thing is for the birds."

"It's Ezell and Uncle John!" I yelled as I dashed to the door to greet them. Aunt Nettie was behind me.

Ezell had stopped at the hospital to pick up Uncle John. Uncle John had to go to bed, though, because of the doctor's orders. He was to have three weeks of bed rest before doing anything else.

Before telling us that he and Ezell had some business to discuss, Uncle John told everyone present that I had saved his life. I didn't quite know what to say to that, so I kept quiet, hoping that he had not heard me yelling and threatening and trying to kill Luther Weems, before taking him to the hospital. Aunt Nettie would have been mortified had she ever heard about it too.

Next thing I knew, the room was being cleared for Uncle John, Ezell, and Mr. Noland, the plantation owner. Uncle John said he had talked to Mr. Noland about what kind of person Ezell was and what he had taught him over the years. Uncle John was able to convince Mr. Noland that Ezell would do just as well as Uncle John running the plantation.

After the talk with Uncle John and Ezell, Mr. Noland called a meeting with his workers to let them know that they were to have a new manager for two months while Uncle John recovered.

Meanwhile, Sheriff Brentman had led his small group of men into the woods and had discovered the body of the man in a shallow grave. This was the second crime scene to be roped off and carefully investigated, and it took quite a few hours too.

Later, we heard that Sheriff Brentman had found something else very important, but none of us knew what that something was or what else had been discovered that morning besides the body of a man.

Sheriff Brentman and his men knew how to keep everything that had any bearing on the crime very quiet. Later, we were all informed that Luther had been found dead and his body had been removed and taken to the coroner's office. The colored people had been right after all in thinking that Luther was in the woods. They just didn't know he had been dead and buried.

"Rose won't have to worry about Ezell now. I need to call and tell her," I said to Aunt Nettie.

CHAPTER FIFTEEN

Micah's Trial

On the way to the Monroe County Jail, Micah wanted to tell Sheriff Brentman what had happened. "Do you want to give me your statement, which will be used in court, Micah?" Sheriff Brentman asked.

"Yes, sir, I do." Micah said.

"Then you will need to tell it when we get you to the jail."

"Yes, sir."

Sheriff Brentman told me later that he wanted Micah to understand that whatever he said could be used against him later, during his trial. Thinking that Micah might give this more thought, Sheriff Brentman told Micah to just wait until they got to the jail.

When they arrived at the county jail, Micah still wanted to tell what had happened, so Sheriff Brentman told him to write out his statement. Micah informed the sheriff that he didn't write well enough to do that, so the sheriff told him to tell the deputy, and he would write it down, then read it back to Micah to sign.

Micah could write his name, so he did that. Sheriff Brentman witnessed and signed, so it was then legal. Basically, Micah stated that he hadn't intended to kill Luther, just hurt him enough that he would never shoot anyone again.

"I didn't like what he did to Mr. Oldham at all. He didn't deserve to be hurt, let alone shot. He was a good man to all of us," Micah said. "When I went back to see about Luther, I found him dead, then I got real scared and drug his body into the woods and tried to hide him by digging as much as I could using my hands. Then I piled bushes on top of all that. Since my shovel was at his house and it was getting dark, I decided I better bring the shovel back the next morning and bury Luther deeper."

According to Sheriff Brentman, Micah was taken in front of a justice of the peace and charged with murder, and bond was set at $25,000. A defense lawyer was appointed to represent the suspect, and a primary hearing was set in the justice of peace Court for a later date.

The day of the hearing, the defense attorney and the suspect waved the hearing, and the case was sent to the grand jury. A few weeks later, the grand jury of Monroe County met, and Micah was indicted. Then the case was set in the Monroe County Circuit Court docket for trial on a murder charge. The suspect remained in custody.

Each one of these steps took time, and Micah said it seemed like an eternity before his trial took place. He also said he was ready to die but hoped he wouldn't have to, because of the one person he knew cared so much for him—Annie. He knew she was praying for him every day and that she had, over a short period of time, fallen in love with him, as he had with her. Now he was in a pickle.

Finally, the day of the trial came. The court house parking lot was full of wagons, pickup trucks, mules, and horses, and also crowded with people mulling about. Most of the people were there to support Micah, as they knew him and were hoping he would be given some consideration. They knew he hadn't meant to kill Luther Weems. They also knew what Luther was like, and what Uncle John was like too. Yes, Uncle John was there, along with Aunt Nettie by his side. I was there too. It was a big day and an important event in the lives of many people in Monroe and surrounding counties. Even reporters were there, with their cameras flashing and attempts to interview people outside in the parking lot. One reporter asked Uncle John what he thought of Micah's saying he hadn't meant to kill Luther. Uncle John said, "If Micah said he didn't mean to kill him, then he didn't. The man just doesn't know his own strength, but he does know to tell the truth; you can count on that." The next day, the headline in one of the local newspapers (I don't remember which one) read "Mr. Oldham of Aberdeen states that if Micah Johnson (the suspect) said he didn't mean to kill him, he didn't."

The court went into session as they called the suspect's name and his attorney to answer the charge of murder. The defense attorney said his client wished to enter a plea of guilty to the charge, but asked for mercy from the court. The judge asked to meet with the defense attorney and the district attorney in his chambers. After a few minutes, they all returned to the courtroom. Excitement was running high in the courtroom, and the judge had to call, "Order," to warn the people to be quiet or they would be removed from the courtroom by the sheriff. Even though the tension was still high, the room became very quiet.

After listening to the district attorney and the defense attorney, the judge made a ruling: "After hearing both sides of the case from the district attorney and the defense attorney, the court finds the suspect guilty of manslaughter. The sentence under Mississippi law is ten to fifteen years, with possible parole after seven years, pending good behavior. The suspect is to be transported to the state penitentiary within ten days. The court is now adjourned."

Some of the people standing just outside of the courtroom then clapped their hands, saying it was a good day for the suspect, as they thought he got a fair hearing and sentence. The parking lot erupted when they heard that the judge had given the suspect a fair hearing. Annie concluded her prayer session with a "Thank you, God! Amen."

CHAPTER SIXTEEN

Past, Present, and Future

$\mathcal{E}$arly that morning, Mr. Noland sent the word out for all of the fieldhand workers to be over at the big house the next day at 7:00 a.m. for an important meeting. He checked to be sure everyone was there, then he proceeded with the meeting. "Attention, everybody! Most you all know Ezell Jefferson Oldham, who has been in the military for the last three years. Mr. Oldham taught Ezell all he knew about running a plantation and keeping the farm equipment running for over ten years before Ezell left to go to war. Now Ezell's back with us, and he's a war hero. He's going to be filling in for Mr. Oldham for a couple of months, until Mr. Oldham is able to go back to work. So for those few of you who might not know him, let me present Ezell Jefferson Oldham, your temporary manager. Now, let's keep this quiet, boys and girls."

Quickly, Ezell began to speak: "I know this is very unusual, but we are all going to pull together and give it our best. We will make Mr. Noland here, as well as Mr. Oldham, proud of us. My plans are to do my very best, and I'll expect no more or no less from you. I believe in management by example, and I'll be right out here with you every single day during this two-month period. Mr. Noland has assigned me to your only empty house, and you all know which one that is, so if you have questions or need to talk to me about anything, before or after work, that's where I'll be. I'm your boss now, so let's get busy."

Ezell couldn't wait for the day to be over so he could go to the big house to call Rose and give her the news. He hadn't known of anyone who was colored before who had been a substitute manager of a plantation. Now to get to a phone to tell Rose …

Rose was, of course, just as pleased as Ezell was about being able to help his papa. Somehow, it seemed to make up for the fact that Ezell was not able to participate in the statewide parade held in Jackson, the state capitol, for the returning veterans and heroes of World War II.

In fact, very few—just a token number, really—of the colored veterans participated in the parade. To me, this was another one of the sad things about the war, that the colored soldiers were fighting for freedom on two fronts and given so little credit at home. Although, when Ezell stood before the farm workers in Prairie, Mississippi, I could see the pride in the expression on his face. Such a joy to see.

Those two months seemed to fly by for Ezell. The workers did very well under his supervision, and he enjoyed the work for the majority of the time. "Hard work," he told himself, "is good for a man." The men gave him a superior rating for Mr. Noland, and the farm's production went higher than it had ever been.

Uncle John had been offered a much better-paying job as a plantation manager in Arkansas for the following year and was discussing it with Mr. Noland. Mr. Noland understood that Uncle John wanted to take the new job for several reasons, and not just the money alone, as he was getting close to his retirement years. Mr. Noland actually encouraged Uncle John to take it because he would not be able to come near matching it monetarily, he told Uncle John. Besides this, he was extremely impressed with the money Ezell was making for him on his land.

And so it was in the early winter of 1945 that Uncle John and Aunt Nettie moved to a larger plantation in Arkansas. This, of course, left Mr. Noland once again without a manager. He thought long and hard about keeping Ezell as his manager. He was concerned about what his friends might think, whether the bank would be willing to grant him his yearly loan, and a dozen other things. Considering all of these things against the difference in the amount of money that Ezell's management would bring in each year, Mr. Noland decided to ask Ezell to stay on as his manager. They could just keep it low-key, he thought, and he could tell his friends, as well as the banker, that he was managing it himself. All he had to do was show up on the farm a little more often and be around more.

Yes, he would ask Ezell to stay on. Of course, he wouldn't pay him as much as he had offered Mr. Oldham, but he would keep him on one way or another. Now to talk to him. Maybe he could set it up for this Saturday, when Ezell was working on the workers' time sheets and paychecks, which Mr. Noland had always signed.

Saturday came, and Mr. Noland began the conversation with Ezell. "Ezell, you have done good work for the past two months, so I want to talk with you about becoming full-time manager of the plantation. If you decide to take the job, I want you to know I won't be able to pay you as much as I told Mr. Oldham I would pay him for next year, but it should be enough for just two people to live on pretty well. So what do you think about it, Ezell?"

"Thank you for considering me, Mr. Noland," Ezell said. "I'm grateful to you. Of course I would have to ask my wife to give up her teaching job and paycheck in Cleveland and come here to live. I would like to make enough money at my job here to be able to ask her to do that, and I sure don't want her to think I'm a fool, being as I have a good-paying job waiting for me in Cleveland that pays as much as her salary and mine together. Now, if you could see to it to pay me the same amount of money you had offered Mr. Oldham, she just might be willing to come here to live, and of course, I would be a lot more inclined to stay on and work here then."

Mr. Norton scratched his head awhile before saying, "Ezell, I'll tell you what. I am willing to do that if it will help you get that woman over here." He continued, "You know about all those nice stacks of boards in the shed out behind the barn? Well, how about if I let you have them to make that little house you're in a lot warmer for the wintertime? There's some cans of paint you can use on the house to paint some trim, or whatever you want, on it too."

"Mr. Noland, you know how much I like working here, in the part of Mississippi that's always been my home, but I can't just ask my wife to—"

"Ezell, I didn't finish what else I was going to tell you. There's also some furniture in one of the other sheds that I keep locked up because I was planning on selling it. Since my wife doesn't plan on using it anymore, I'll even let you have that, just to make your place look more like

Ezell's tenant house before repairs

a woman would like for it to look. Can't do much more for you than that, Ezell."

"Except for what I need to be able to stay here," Ezell said rather dejectedly under his breath.

"What were you saying just then, Ezell?"

"Oh, not much, Mr. Noland, just that my wife, Rose, is a teacher, and when we talked all of this over a few nights ago, she mentioned that she would like teach some of the younger children on the plantation here how to read, write, and do numbers—if you were interested in that, since most of the plantations have schools now. That would be up to you, of course. So what do you think, Mr. Noland?"

"I think you drive a hard bargain, Ezell," Mr. Noland replied, "and you got the money your wife wanted you to get too. I also think you and your wife are going to be worth every penny of it. It's a deal."

"Thank you, Mr. Noland. I'll let Rose know right away."

Now Ezell really had something to tell Rose, a good first-year salary, as well as being the first colored plantation manager in the state of Mississippi. It's hard to believe, but "Glory be, my Lord has moved again."

*****

"Rose, darling, I have some good news. Are you sitting down? You and I can afford to live together now. I was offered the job as a full-time plantation manager here at Southville."

"Are you serious, Ezell? Do you have it on paper? How much will you make? Enough for us to have children and send them through school?"

"Rose, one question at a time. I know you are excited and happy, and so am I, but calm down and I'll tell you!"

"Ezell, think of what this means for our people—our kind. You're opening a door, my love!" Rose exclaimed.

On and on the phone conversation went between the newlyweds. "God was good," Ezell said.

The next Saturday, Mr. Noland brought Ezell the written contract, and the two signed it. Both men felt good about what was done that day.

Rose decided that it was now time for her to give up her job in Cleveland and move to Southville where Ezell was.

Meanwhile, Ezell had been working hard to repair the little house, even putting on a new roof and painting it. He went to the co-op place in Aberdeen and bought some little plants to put in front of the house. Ezell sanded all of the wooden furniture and either varnished or painted it. Many of the pieces needed repairing, and he did that, as well as arranging everything in the house as best as he knew how. The house was cleaned, floors scrubbed, and walls painted in anticipation of Rose's arrival.

The final thing Ezell wanted to do before Rose's arrival was to find just the right swing for them. And who was the best carpenter and woodworking man he knew? Mr. Paul Jefferson in West Point. That night, Ezell called his biological father and told him the good news. After that, he asked him about doing a special swing for him and Rose. Of course, Paul was delighted and quickly set about using his woodworking skills to create the best, as well as the prettiest, swing he had ever done. Paul made and used decorative knobs on top of the swing, and when he finished with all the woodwork, he sanded and varnished it so that it would last for many years. He wanted it to not only be comfortable for the couple, for his son, but the nicest-looking swing anybody had ever seen. And indeed it was. Ezell told Uncle John that it was fit for a queen—Queen Rose it was called from then on.

Rose loved it and enjoyed sitting in it every day when Ezell came in and their work was done. It became a kind of ritual for them, as they sat and talked over their day.

One afternoon, there was an exceptionally beautiful sunset. The entire sky seemed to be a painted canvas starting just above the flat horizon line at the end of the prairie grasslands. It was obviously done by the greatest of all the world's painters—the Master Artist. Rose had never seen anything in her life so beautiful, and that night she was hurrying Ezell to finish his bath and come out to the swing with her. She had put on her prettiest dress, combed her hair away from her face, and tried to compensate for her slightly protruding belly. She wanted to look pretty for Ezell on the night she was going to tell him that she was with child.

Ezell finally came out and sat down with her. She gave Ezell a tall glass of cool Artisian water that bubbled up from the spring near their house. She sipped from her own glass of cool water. Rose tried to divert his gaze to the gorgeous sunset until he told her plainly that he wanted to keep on looking at her because he thought she was so much more beautiful than any sunset. So Rose became quiet and continued to gaze at the sunset while Ezell continue to gaze at her, and he thanked God that they were together now, as well as for all the other blessings. There were far too many for any one man to begin to deserve.

So this is what it feels like when the Lord *bona fides* a man, Ezell thought. All the puffin, strutting, and pretending what you ain't is gone—just GONE, with all its grief and loneliness. What's left is only what He made in His own image, just like the Bible says. Glory Be! Now I know what it's like to belong in this world with all of the different races of people. Most of them will accept me as I am, and if they don't, it's all right because my Heavenly Father, the maker of us all, does; and I do too. It really is like being born all over again. I've got to tell Rose, but how do I do that, Lord? How can I tell her that you bonafied me?

Ezell prayed silently for a while before he turned to Rose. "I gave my life to Him, that was all—and that was so small, and look at all He gave to me. My past is redeemed, my present makes sense, and my future is secure. I no longer need to be right, first, recognized, praised, regarded, or rewarded. I'm finished and done with low-life living, colorless dreams, worldly talking, cheap giving, and dwarfed goals. I won't take back, let up, slow down, back away, or be still. I now live by faith. I labor with power from above. I want to use myself up for all He has given to me."

Rose thought this might be the time to tell Ezell her news. "Ezell dear, you may want to save a bit of yourself for our child." She began to softly pat her newly rounded little belly.

Section
II

OLD-TIMEY EATIN'

Ezell's Favorite Foods

Please remember that Ezell had not only Annie's soul food but Aunt Nettie's gourmet-like cooking from which to choose his favorite foods. Since I didn't want to turn this into a cookbook, I selected for Ezell only a few of those wonderful old-timey foods he requested enough times that I knew for sure they were his favorites. In fact, I started out with well over fifty of them, and I kept cutting them down to the ones that are listed here.

I hope you enjoy these great dishes as much as we did and will maybe want to prepare them for special occasions too. Just tell your guests that they are old-timey recipes. (Ezell's favorites from the book on your coffee table, *A Man Named Ezell*).

BEVERAGES

SPEARMINT ICED TEA

1 cup washed mint
1/2 tea-holder dry tea leaves
6-8 cups water
3/4 cup sugar

1. Boil a good-size handful of mint taken from the garden. Wash it well to get the dust off. After it's boiled for 15-20 minutes, set it off the stove to cool.

2. Prepare the boiling water to go into a teapot. Put tea into a tea-holder (a small ball or cylinder) and drop it into the teapot. Allow it to steep for about 15 minutes, then remove the tea holder. Be sure the tea is dark enough; if not, put the tea ball back in for a while.

3. Lift the sprigs of spearmint, or any mint, and squeeze all of the juice out of the leaves. Take all of the floating leaves out and pour the liquid into the teapot. Add some sugar and stir.

INSTANT HOT CHOCOLATE

1 lb. powdered milk
1 lb. Hershey's instant cocoa
1 cup powdered sugar
1 small jar Cremona (non-dairy creamer)
1 3-oz. box instant chocolate pudding mix

Mix together and store in a tight container. Use 1/4 cup mix to 1 cup hot water. Top with marshmallows, if desired.

VEGETABLES

FRESH GREEN BEANS

1 large bunch green greens (string or snap)
1 large pot of boiling water
1 large pot of ice water
2 tsp olive oil
Lemon juice
Salt and pepper

1. Get a nice-size bundle of fresh green beans (preferably out of your own garden). Wash them well and remove the strips. Have a big pot of water boiling with a strainer in it and another large pot full of ice water.

2. A few minutes before dinner is to be served, drop the green beans into the pot of boiling water and let it come back to a boil. Note time on the clock, or use a timer, and boil for 6 minutes. Timing is important if you want the green beans crisp and not soft.

3. After 6 minutes is reached, take the pot over to the sink, lift the strainer, and plunge it directly into the ice water to stop the cooking process. Leave the green beans in the ice water until they have cooled, then put them in a nice serving dish with a bit of olive oil, lemon juice, salt, and pepper. Enjoy!

MAKE-AHEAD MASHED POTATOES

6 lbs. potatoes, peeled and cut into wedges

1 package (8 oz.) cream cheese, cubed

2 large egg whites, beaten

1 cup (8 oz.) sour cream

1/4 cup onion, grated or chopped very fine

1 teaspoon salt

1/2 teaspoon pepper

2 tablespoon, melted butter

1. Place potatoes in a Dutch oven or large pan and cover with water, then bring to a boil. Reduce heat, cover, and cook 20–30 minutes or until tender. Drain.

2. In a large bowl, mash potatoes with cream cheese. Combine beaten egg whites, sour cream, onions, salt, and pepper. Stir into potatoes until blended. Transfer to a large baking dish—3 or 4 quarts. Drizzle with butter. Cover and refrigerate overnight.

3. Remove from the refrigerator 30 minutes before baking. Preheat oven to 350F. Cover and bake for 55 minutes. Uncover and bake 5–7 minutes longer or until thermometer reads 160F. Don't brown on top.

OLD-FASHIONED TURNIP GREENS

5 lbs. fresh greens with roots
1/2 lb. salt pork, or cubes of ham
6 to 8 cups of water
2 Tbsp. bacon drippings
Green onion (optional)

1. After picking and washing turnip greens three times, tear into bite-size pieces. Take out big stems.
2. Rinse salt pork and cut into 2-inch pieces, or cut from the top down to the skin leaving 1/2 inch slices intact.
3. Peel the turnip roots and slice.
4. Combine salt pork and water in a large Dutch oven. Bring to a boil. Cover, reduce heat, and simmer for 30 minutes. If your family likes, add 2 Tbsp. bacon drippings and green onions, as well as a little apple cider to taste.

REALLY GOOD BLACK-EYED PEAS

12 slices of bacon
1 large bowl fresh peas (2lb can)
1/2 cup broth

1. Before beginning with the black-eyed peas, cook a pan of very lean bacon until it is crisp. Crumble a bit and set aside.
2. Use black-eyed peas, frozen or canned. If canned, rinse out most of the salt.
3. Cook for about 10 minutes on top of the stove in a boiler. Add broth, maybe 1/2 cup or a little more, or some water. Then crumble bacon over the top and serve while warm.

MAIN DISHES

BAKED HAM

According to Aunt Nettie, it was important to obtain the finest Tennessee or Virginia smoked Ham and bake it in an earthen-covered dish, if at all possible. It was also important to cook for the correct number of hours per pound of meat.

8-10 lb. ham
1 to 1 1/2 cups apple cider
Parsley

1. Bake the ham in apple cider until tender.
2. When done and cooled a little, take off the skin carefully and put cut paper around the "knuckles" or twist a tuft of fringed paper around the knuckles. Place plenty of parsley around the dish. This will always ensure an "inviting appearance," Aunt Nettie said.

Uncle John carved the ham with a sharp, thin knife, first around it almost to midway, then across the other (long) way. He said the slices should be even and thin, cutting both lean and fat together—always down to the bone.

HAM GRAVY

1 – 2 cups ham drippings
1 Tbsp. flour
1 tsp water

1. Mix a bit of flour (1 Tbsp.) with a small amount of water (1 tsp. or less) so a smooth paste can be made.
2. Place 1 or 2 cups of ham drippings into a medium-size frying pan and bring almost to a boil (unless it's thick, then just heat it very slowly).
3. Mix in the flour-water paste and stir continuously.
4. Simmer (about a minute), then cool and taste.
    a. If it needs more flour, add a little. Add a butter cube and stir again.
    b. If it's too dry, gradually stir in a bit more water.
    c. If it's too wet, do the paste again and gradually stir in the ham drippings, as above, so it won't be lumpy.

If combined with sliced ham, this and some biscuits make a very nice breakfast for the next morning. Be sure to make some grits. In fact, this menu is good for any meal time.

CHICKEN AND DUMPLINGS

Chicken Base:
4 large chicken breasts or 1 small whole chicken
1/2 large onion, chopped
1 cup milk
2 cans cream of chicken soup
5 ribs of celery
1/4 tsp. dill weed
1/2 tsp. parsley salt
Salt and pepper to taste

Feather Dumplings:
Makes 8 servings
2 cups flour
4 tsp. baking powder
1/4 tsp. white or black pepper
1 tsp. salt
1 egg, beaten well
2 tbs. melted butter
2/3 cup milk

1. Cook chicken in a big pot with 5 cups of water and seasoning and chopped up celery.
2. Sauté onion in a frying pan with a good amount of oil until it is tender and browned.
3. Then, to the pot of water, add chicken and seasoning.
4. After 20 minutes of medium-to-slow boiling, take chicken out and debone it, chop into approximately 1-inch cubes.
5. Return chicken to large boiler and bring to a boil. Gradually add cans of soup and cup of milk, and boil slowly. Cover and cook on low for another 15–20 minutes. Move off heat and let cool some before straining the fat off.
6. Heat the broth and chicken again.

7. The feather dumplings could be prepared in advance or may be prepared now, while the chicken and broth are reheating to a slow boil. Mix up feather dumplings by sifting dry ingredients together. Add egg, melted butter, and enough milk to make a moist, stiff batter. Drop by teaspoons into boiling liquid.

8. Slowly add dumplings, one at a time, returning to a boil after each. Letting the dumplings sit for 20 minutes is the secret to having good, light dumplings, so take your time in adding the dumplings to the boiling mix.

PORK TENDERLOIN ROAST

6–8 lb. pork tenderloin
Salt
Pepper
12–15 yams, peeled and cut into pieces
8–12 apples, cored and quartered
2 1/2 cups orange juice
1 1/4 cups brown sugar

1. Salt and pepper tenderloin. Bake at 425F for 30-45 minutes.
2. Add yams, apples, orange juice, and brown sugar. Cover with foil and bake for 3 hours, or more if needed for tenderness (400F for the first 1 1/2 hours, then at 350F for the next 1 and 1/2 hours). Delicious!

BREADS

BUTTERMILK BISCUITS

Makes 14 biscuits

2 1/2 cups all-purpose flour
1 Tbsp. plus 1 tsp. baking powder
1/2 tsp. baking soda
1/4 tsp. salt
1/4 cup plus 2 Tbsp. shortening
1 cup buttermilk

1. Combine flour, baking powder, soda, and salt. Mix well.
2. Cut in shortening with a pastry blender until mixture resembles coarse meal.
3. Add buttermilk, stirring just until dry ingredients are moistened.
4. Turn dough out onto a floured surface. Knead 3 or 4 times.
5. Roll dough to 1/2-inch thickness. Cut straight down with a biscuit cutter (2 1/2 inch cutter) don't twist.
6. Place biscuits on a greased baking sheet. Bake at 420F for 10 minutes or until tops are golden.

BISCUITS AND GRAVY

2 1/2 cup flour (Martha White, if available)
1 tsp. salt
1/2 tsp. soda
2 tsp. baking powder
3 Tbsp. shortening
1 cup buttermilk

1. Preheat oven to 425F.
2. Sift flour and dry ingredients together.
3. Work in shortening, then add buttermilk slowly, mixing well.
4. Roll out on lightly floured board.
5. Cut into shapes and bake for 10–12 minutes. Be sure to cut dough straight down; don't twist, with the cutter.

SOUTHERN CRUSTY CORNBREAD

Makes 8 servings

1 cup cornmeal
1/2 cup all-purpose flour
1 tsp. sugar
1 Tbsp. baking powder
1/2 tsp. baking soda
1/2 tsp. salt
1 egg, beaten
1 cup buttermilk
1/2 cup bacon drippings

1.   Preheat oven to 425F.
2.   Combine first six dry ingredients; mix well.
3.   Add egg and buttermilk. Stir until smooth.
4.   Place bacon drippings in a 9-inch cast-iron skillet at 425F for 5 minutes.
5.   Remove skillet from oven and quickly pour batter into the skillet. Bake at 425F for 20–25 minutes or until golden.

Note: If one wants cornbread for supper that night, it would be a good idea to make an extra pan of muffins or corn sticks.

YEAST ROLLS

1 cup milk

3/4 cup sugar

2 packages yeast

6 cups unsifted flour

1 cup lukewarm water

1 tsp. salt

2 sticks butter

2 eggs, beaten

1. Put 1 cup milk on stove to heat, coming barely to a boil.
2. Dissolve yeast in lukewarm water. Do not stir for 10 minutes, then stir well.
3. Cream butter with sugar, and pour hot milk over it. Mix thoroughly and let cool.
4. Sift together flour and salt.
5. Pour yeast into butter mix, add beaten eggs, and then flour. Beat thoroughly. Cover and refrigerate for 12 hours.
6. Place rolls in pan and let rise for 2 hours before baking.
7. Bake in 400F oven for 12–15 minutes.

Freezes well after baking, or covered dough may be kept in refrigerator for about a week (but punch down once a day).

DESSERTS

SMALL, QUICK PEACH COBBLER

1 can freestone peaches or 5 fresh peaches

1/2 cup self-rising flour

1/2 stick margarine

1/2 cup sugar

1.   Pour fruit into 1-quart buttered casserole dish.

2.   Mix flour and sugar together and sprinkle over fruit.

3.   Cut margarine into slices over top.

4.   Bake in 350F oven for 1 hour.

5.   Serve plain or with ice cream or whipped cream.

Note: To make a regular pie, use following ingredients:

2 cans freestone peaches or 10 medium sized fresh peaches

1 cup self-rising flour

1 stick butter

1 tsp. vanilla extract

1 cup sugar

CHOCOLATE CHIP COOKIES

Makes 3 dozen cookies

2 sticks unsalted butter
1 tsp. vanilla
3/4 cup sugar
2 3/4 cups flour
3/4 cup brown sugar
1 tsp. soda
2 eggs
1 tsp. salt
1/2 tsp. water
12 oz. chocolate chips

1. Cream butter, sugar, eggs, water, and vanilla.
2. Add flour, soda, and salt. Blend well.
3. Stir in chocolate chips.
4. Bake at 350F for 10–12 minutes.

RHUBARB PIE

Rhubarb to fill a 1 quart bowl – about 8 stalks
1 cup sugar
1/4 tsp salt
1/2 tsp nutmeg
2 egg whites beaten
2 Tbsp. flour
1/2 loaf white bread

1. Cut the large stalks off where the leaves commence, strip off the outside skin, and then cut the stalks in pieces 1/2 inch long.
2. Line a big casserole dish with buttered, toasted white bread, toasted lightly on both sides with the layer of crust off trimmed all the way around on each piece of bread. (You could also cut the bread into even cubes and layer them. The original recipe, however, from Kentucky during the 1800s, did not do this.)
3. Whichever way you decide, brush beaten egg whites on both sides of the toast.
4. To a 1-quart bowl of cut rhubarb, add 2 cups of sugar mixed with 1/4 tsp. salt, a little nutmeg, and two Tbsp. flour.
5. Layer toast, rhubarbs, and sugar mixture.
6. Bake in a quick oven until the pie loosens from the dish. (Note: For this day and time, the oven temperature should be set at 350F, and the pie should be cooked for around 50 minutes. You could also sprinkle more sugar on top of the pie in the last few minutes of baking. Be sure the rhubarb is tender too! I use about 1/2 a loaf of white bread to 7–8 medium-length stalks.)
7. After the pie is almost baked, place aluminum foil over the dish to keep it from getting too brown. Rhubarb pies made in this way are far superior to those made by the fruit being stewed.

APPLE FRITTERS

2 cups all-purpose flour
2 tsp baking powder
1 tsp salt
1/2 cup non-fat dry milk powder
1/3 cup sugar
1/2 tsp cinnamon
2 eggs
1 cup water
2 cups peeled, grated apples
Powdered sugar (optional)

1. Mix together flour, baking powder, salt, dry milk, sugar and cinnamon.
2. Mix eggs and water, add to flour mixture, stir until flour is just dampened.
3. Fold in grated apples
4. Fry at 375F. Drop from well-rounded teaspoon into hot fat. Fry until golden on both sides, turning once.
5. Drain well on paper towel.
6. Roll in powdered sugar or glaze (optional)

GLAZE - APPLE FRITTER

1 box powdered sugar
1 Tbsp. cornstarch
1 Tbsp. melted butter
1 Tbsp. sweet cream
1 tsp vanilla
Water

1. Mix all ingredients together.
2. Add water in small portions until desired consistence.
3. Dip hot fritters into glaze and place on a rack to dry.

Extra glaze can be used on baked apples or another pastry.

A Word from the Author:

A *Man Named Ezell* is a mostly true story. Ezell was a wonderful man, adopted by my beloved Uncle John and Aunt Nettie in a time when such things were considered taboo. Thankfully, social morals and attitudes have changed since the 1940s, and for the better. Terms considered offensive today, Japs, colored, etc. are used in the text because they were prevalent at the time of this story.

Many resources were used in researching this novel. Among them, *Flag of Our Fathers* by James D. Bradley, *Tennozan: The Battle of Okinawa and the Atomic Bomb* by George Feifer, *Iwo Jima: Legacy of Valor* by Bill D. Ross, *With the Old Breed: At Peleliu and Okinawa* by E.B. Sledge and *Guadalcanal Diary* by Richard Tregaskis.

While doing research, I came across *The Island of the Damned* by R. V. Burgin. Burgin said that the war was a waste and the Battle of Peleliu was the toughest battle of the Pacific War. It was a battle that never should have been fought. MacArthur wanted the infantry on Peleliu surrounded, but the Allies had already bombed the airfield there months before. There was no way the Japanese could have rebuilt it to make it invisible again. They were pretty much finished as an airpower.

In 1995, I had the opportunity to live in American Samoa; a true cultural eye-opener. I enjoyed every minute of it, learning much from the experience. Such as: the letters in the Samoan alphabet are so few, many words served two purposes. Likewise, a word was often used one time for a particular item and two times to mean another thing. An example is lava and lava-lava. This was explained to me by the young Samoan man, Tavita, who was my husband's work/study student.

Tavita, age twenty, had declared that he liked our home much better than the thatched-roof building made of a few palm trees, leaves, and poles and a dirt floor in which he lived. Our home was very close to a typical Western home. It was made from cinder blocks, lumber, and had running water and electricity. In it, there was an extra twin bed, ice cream in the refrigerator most of the time, and a reasonably good mother substitute for him. That, of course, was me. I was his "Mama Jo," who cooked, washed and ironed his clothes, and taught him about the ways of American students who were about his age.

We learned so much from Tavita about the Samoan ways of life and of how they really felt and thought. It was truly education beyond a textbook about native Samoan people, who were in many ways people with the same hopes and dreams, desires, wishes, wants, and needs as ours, but at the same time quite different in their thinking and behavior, even to their sense of humor.

Ezell's final thoughts as he sits with Rose at the end of the novel, although paraphrased, are taken from a prayer said by a young pastor in Zimbabwe, Africa, who was martyred for his faith. *Now What?: God's Guide to Life for Graduates* by John Ortberg.

CPSIA information can be obtained
at www.ICGtesting.com
Printed in the USA
LVHW05s1102260718
584939LV00004B/4/P